ANCHOR

Book Three in The Wake Series

Book formatting by Stacey Blake, Champagne Formats
Editing by Marion Making Manuscripts, makingmanuscripts.com

ISBN-13: 978-1511792578
ISBN-10: 1511792574

Other Books

Fade In

The Wake Series

Bait

Sail

Anchor

The Very Second Time coming Late 2015

For star-crossed lovers

under cloudy skies

who never give up on love.

PROLOGUE

Blake

C*ASEY WAS WAITING FOR me. He was meeting my mom and dad.*

"No, I think you're going to stay and tell me what I did that was *so* bad you had to fuck another guy the whole time we were married."

I didn't say anything else. I simply turned on my heels for the door.

"You can't leave without your precious papers, Blake. Your divorce papers."

"Please, just let me go," I begged.

"I'm not sure if I'm ready to let you leave just yet. Let's go get those papers."

He began to pull me up the stairs.

Casey, I need you.

"You want to go? This isn't like me? I gave you everything. You didn't have to work and travel like you were. You could've had a good life here with me. We could've had a family."

Pain. My arm. My heart.

Grant never knew me, proven by the harsh fact, he was a complete stranger. How had I been so naive? Reality's punch to my gut was brutal, rivaling the pain I was feeling.

"But, no. I wasn't good enough, so you fucked someone else. So this is the new me, Blake. Maybe you'll like me better this way."

Step after step, he went backward, jerking me as he went, his force only waning when I struggled against his hold. I fought and pulled back, almost bringing us both down. He stopped, grabbed a fistful of my hair, and heaved me up toward him.

"Does he pull your hair? Is that it?"

Casey is waiting for me. What if he thinks I've changed my mind?

What if he leaves?

A fleeting surge of adrenaline spiked through my system. I had one more shot. I didn't overthink it; there wasn't time. I lunged forward, taking him off guard since he was pulling me. Head first into his thigh—which was the closest part of him I could reach—and I bit him. My teeth dug through the denim of his jeans until I felt his skin break in my mouth. Until I tasted blood. Metallic and salty.

"You fucking bitch!" he screamed.

I was free.

I heard Casey's voice, he was with me. So close. I felt his warmth surround me.

"I want you tonight. You've got something I need. I don't know what it is. I'm probably crazy. Humor me though. Be with me."

I leaned back. I was falling. I was going to him.

"You might marry him today. But the brave fighter in here—she's mine. She always will be. Love doesn't give a fuck about a piece of paper. When are you going to realize that this isn't just love? There isn't even a word for this.*"*

Words from our past were new in my ears as I weightlessly fell into nothingness.

I'm dreaming of you, Lou.

Someone was talking. Their voice was muffled … like through a pillow.

Casey. I was trying to get to you. I'm trying to get to you.

Darkness.

ONE

Blake

Sunday, June 13, 2010

"WHEN YOU WAKE UP, you should probably go ahead and ask me to marry you," I whispered in the dark to a man who—quite literally—owned my heart. Fair and square. There was a nightlight on in my bathroom down the hall, but other than that it was completely dark and quiet. When I'd woken up, from thoughts I still wouldn't allow myself to think about—*when I had the choice*—I was sweaty, in a warm bed with Casey. Except, not in the way I would prefer to be.

Over the past week I'd been in a haze from the strong pain-killers, and I was still sleeping at the weirdest times even though they'd all but worn off by then. However groggy, and regardless of the hour, every time I woke up, he was there ready to talk. Ready to make me laugh. Bring me something to drink. Feed me to the point of nausea.

He seemed calm, which I was thankful for in that moment. Relaxed and peaceful. He needed rest, and I felt obligated to leave him alone, so he could catch up on the sleep I knew I'd deprived him of. He had to be exhausted. He was always awake when I was.

So I lay there absorbing him and reflected. My heart rate slowed from the dream as I let my mind wander around our new reality.

I'd been home for a few days. It was Sunday—I think.

Days blended together. I measured time by what television shows were on and what he was trying to feed me. Breakfast. *The Today Show*. Lunch. He was watching a cooking show. Dinner. The news. If it weren't for those minor clues, and the light from the sun and moon filtering in from outside, I'd have no clue what time it was at all.

It was dark out when he carried me to bed. My bed? Our bed? There was so much that wasn't clear. So much that needed discussing. Defined. Lines needed to be drawn. Sad as it was, I was still nervous that it could get worse before better. Would Grant cause more trouble? Would I have to go through a trial? I wanted to sever myself from the past, not continue living in it. My mind traveled into dark corners, so I focused my thoughts on *him*.

The beautiful man beside me. His physical appearance and the word 'beautiful' were exclusive. It was everything about him. His kindness. Passion. He loved me unconditionally. Goodness oozed from him and coated everything it touched. Including me.

I needed him forever.

I'd consistently asked him, twice a day it seemed, if he'd marry me. Persistent and stubborn, he'd say, "I'm asking *you*, honeybee. But thank you. And I *will* marry you."

That was the same thing as a yes. Right?

My heart, and everything else, belonged to him. I had already been his for such a long time. I refused to wait any longer.

He loved me. I loved him.

I was single—for all intents and purposes—and he was free.

I wasn't going to waste another minute not letting him know I was there for the taking. If he wanted me. Every part of me belonged to every part of him. My lips were the mate to his. My arms fit around him like wrapping paper on Christmas presents. My thoughts were stained with him, the same as my heart. My eyes never failed to look for his. The view was always such a nice bonus.

"You know you want to. Just ask me," I quietly pleaded. "I'll say yes, and we'll run away." That was something of a fantasy. But who doesn't dream about being swept away by the man they're in love with?

With all of the stealth and speed of a geriatric sloth, I moved away from him to take a little walk around the house. Maybe there was something on television that would hold my attention. I gently slid my feet off the side of the bed, then felt his hand find mine.

"Where ya goin'?" he asked. His voice was gravelly and thick with sleep. I glanced over my shoulder. I smiled because his eyes weren't even open. It was possible he wasn't even awake. Bringing my leg back up on the bed, I ran my hand over his chest and felt him breathing just as softly and evenly as before.

"Casey?"

I waited, but there was nothing.

I was sucked back into him. I didn't need a walk. I needed his touch.

My fingers journeyed to their favorite playground—his hair. I combed through it softly and as curly hairs pulled away from each other, they fluffed up. The contrast of his dark hair against the creamy white pillowcase allowed me to see the effect I was having on it. Puffy hair and all, he still looked handsome.

Through everything, he'd been exactly what I'd needed.

He didn't speak carefully to me like I was glass. But his touch, although still holding the heat that had always been there, felt cooler. Somewhat reserved. My body was still healing, so I could understand his hesitancy to go crazy. Still, I missed the feel of him. The way my blood and muscles felt new after the rush of pleasure he gave me.

He could heal me, distract me. Replace hurt with desire. Fear with ecstasy. Hate with love. Greedily, I just couldn't resist him. I supposed it was typical. When it came right down to it, I'd always been selfish, but this time I wanted to please and give more than I took.

I changed course. I crawled back onto the bed closer to him and, carefully, wrapped my leg over his side-laying body.

I cinched closer. He reflexively drew me near and a moan rumbled in his throat.

"You're starting trouble, honeybee," he said as he rolled onto his back taking me with him. I lay on his chest, legs straddling him. Even though his head was foggy, his body was awake. Evident by the hardness I felt when I stretched to kiss his mouth. Not just for his lips, but for the friction created by sliding against him.

"You don't have to wake up. I can do this on my own," I assured him sarcastically. "You just fall back asleep. Nothing to see here."

"I was dreaming about this." He shifted under me and the darker thoughts I'd had earlier started to fade. The knot in my belly changed to need.

"Really, which part?"

"You. But you were kissing my neck." He moved his head to the side and I laughed to myself. He invited me to press my lips against the skin under his ear. He tasted sweet and satisfying and better than any meal I'd had in a long time.

"Mmm. Like this?"

His hips rocked and he ran his hands up and down my sides under my tank top. It made me arch into him, and I took liberties, grinding against the glorious piece of man beneath me.

"Yeah. Kinda," he mumbled. "And my mouth." His lips puckered and he gave me a little squeeze. My ribs screamed and my breath caught, the pain surprising me. Out of all of my injuries, my ribs were the worst. He sensed my brief discomfort. "I'm sorry. I wasn't thinking."

He relaxed his hold. The room was barely bright enough for

me to see his worry. I didn't like it. I missed the reckless passion his eyes held only a few weeks ago.

"I'm okay. Please. I'm ready." I snuck a hand between us and stroked him over his briefs. No matter what he said, part of him was ready too.

"Blake, you've only been home a few days. I'm not going anywhere." What he was saying and the way his hips rocked into my hand contradicted each other. He continued, "Don't rush yourself."

"I'm not. I want to." Wanted to? Hell, I *needed* to. I needed to feel good. To be consumed by him. I wanted my lungs heavy with his breath and my ears full of words from his worshiping lips. I wanted there to be, at least, a few peaceful seconds, where I wasn't pretending I couldn't remember what happened at Grant's.

I wanted the calm that came right after we were intimate.

Mostly, I wanted to tell him all of that, but I wasn't sure how to say it. I knew he'd understand. Or try. What were the words for *fix me*? Let's fix this together?

Words failed me, but my hand did not.

I continued to glide over his length, our skin only separated by thin fabric.

"I want that too, but it doesn't have to be tonight. I'm not going anywhere." Casey's words reassured me, but it was short-lived. Anxiety or panic, although quiet, whispered in the background of my mind. *He'll have to go back to San Francisco at some point. Will he stay long? How long will we be apart?*

"But what about when you do go? You'll have to go, won't you? Eventually?" The words spilled out before I could make them yield to my better judgment.

What if Grant came here when Casey was gone?

He sat up in bed and leaned back against the headboard, taking me with him. He embraced me as I naturally lay my head on his bare chest. All heat gone from the moment. My fleeting chance at a diversion from my thoughts, vanished.

"It'll be fine. We're going to be fine."

"I want all of this to be cleaned up. All of the mess I've made to disappear. I want you," I confessed as I searched for clues on his face in the dark. Something reassuring. Something convincing. "How do you know it's all going to be fine?"

"Because you and I, we're workers." His hands ran circles over my back in a slow, soothing pattern.

"Workers? I haven't worked in a week and neither have you." I wasn't following. How was that supposed to make me feel any better?

He laughed at me a little and continued.

"We don't mind work is what I should have said, I suppose. We fell in love. It wasn't the right time. It was inconvenient as fuck and, at times, it hurt so bad. It would have been much easier to quit." His fingers tenderly brushed across my cheek. "You and I are tough, Blake. Even though it probably doesn't feel or look like it, we were fighting to be together that whole time. And we're so close. We're so close I can *feel* it. Look at us. I'm here in your home. In your bed. No one to hide from. No one to tell us it's wrong or tell us we should be anywhere else. I've dreamed of us being like this. Together. I think you have too." His thumb ironed out my brow, releasing the tension I held there.

"I have, but I want to give you more."

"We're both getting more. We're going to have everything."

"Then why can't we just get married and let everything begin now? Today." We'd had this conversation over and over, but Casey was insistent. Like me, I supposed. He wanted it his way.

"Because you deserve more than that. So do I. It would feel cheap to me."

My arm around his neck, I spun his hair around my finger. "Cheap?"

"Yeah. We've been through so much, and now to run off and get married at the courthouse, like we're ashamed—well, it feels wrong. I want to give you things. Things you've never had. And I want to share every precious moment with you that *I've* never had."

"I'm a divorcee," I painfully reminded him.

"I'm sick of hearing that excuse." His hand stilled.

"It's not an excuse. It's the truth. I can't give you my firsts. I gave them to …" I didn't have to finish. I didn't want to finish. The facts made me ill.

"Did you mean it? Did you mean any of it with him?" His voice was still butter-smooth, but he was being firm with me. I liked the feel of the familiar push and pull we were so good at, even if I wasn't sure if I understood his logic.

Memories of my first wedding trickled into my head. Ironically, they all had to do with Casey. Him coming to me that morning. Our fight. Thinking that I'd imagined him at the ceremony.

"I hope you have to pretend it's me to walk down the aisle."

Which I did.

"No," I confessed in the dark. I could give him that. It was true; he was the only man I'd ever wanted to marry. I kissed his chest.

"Then it doesn't fucking count, honeybee. Do you love me?"

I brought my mouth to his and answered, "I do. I love you so much, but I want to show you I'm yours. I want to be yours in every way."

"I want that too. But not out of some sense of obligation. Not because you think you owe me. And don't try to say that's not some of your rush. It is. I know you, Blake. I know how you think. It's a hobby of mine." He kissed my forehead and then my nose. "I'm an expert-level Blake enthusiast."

"Then tell me what *you* want." I climbed closer, desperate to give him something. "Anything. All you have to do is name it."

"Okay." His voice lifted, levity finding him, like he was getting ready to read me his Christmas list. "Okay. I'm going to tell you this stuff, and number one, you can't laugh at me. And number two, you can't freak out and force all of it to happen."

"Okay, tell me."

He cupped my face with his warm palms and pushed his forehead against mine. "Promise. Promise me telling you all of this won't make you crazy."

"I promise. Now get on with it."

"I want to propose to you when it's special. I don't know how. God, I've pictured doing it so many ways." He laughed. "The number of fantasy proposals I've had are starting to rival the other fantasies I have with you."

I giggled. He was cute and the excitement in his voice did make me crazy. He was right. I was going to move heaven and earth to give him everything he wanted. Then I thought, that was kind of perfect. Wasn't that love? Wanting to be and do and give everything you could to make the other's wildest dreams come true?

"What else?" I prodded.

"Did you have a bachelorette party? Because I totally want a bachelor party. One last hurrah, you know?" He rocked into me to let me know he was only half kidding.

"I'll give you one last hurrah."

"And I think I want one of those couple's showers where everyone comes over to one house, or we go out to a restaurant, and they all tell us how cute we are and give us presents. Can we register for stuff? I think we can. Micah and Cory didn't do all that fun shit, but I heard them talking about it. I was like, free shit and a party? Yeah. I'm doing that."

I was mentally taking notes. The positivity poured from him. No more doubts. No more guilt. No more questioning if this was real.

"And for the wedding, I think I want to do something outside." His voice was hesitant, but then he added, "I know what you're thinking and stop. It'll be different than before. And absolutely, under no circumstances, ever, over my dead body will there be violins."

What a shame. I loved violins, but I knew what he was referring to.

"I'll wear a bow tie and you'll look stunning in a paper sack." *Very funny, Mr. Moore.*

"A paper sack?"

I couldn't help it. My mind wandered to my last wedding dress. Fuck lace. Hell, fuck white. Who was I trying to fool?

"Okay, you can wear a dress. Maybe we could have the wedding somewhere in the middle. Like Oregon maybe? Somewhere where *we* own the memories. New memories. Somewhere only ours." He sweetly kissed my cheek.

I liked that idea. I liked all of it. Especially the bow tie.

"And our families and close friends will be there and we'll say what's in our hearts. Then we'll sign papers and you'll change your name to mine."

It sounded like a dream. I wanted everything the way he'd painted the picture in my head. The exact way he was describing. I could see it all.

"I'll take your name." I turned more to face him and slid my hands around to his back.

"You're damn right you will. Blake Moore has *always* sounded good to me."

Me too.

"Then we'll dance all night and then … oh, then you're in for it, Mrs. Moore." My heart raced and my stomach, for the first time in days, completely relaxed. I was getting my very own fairytale in bed, and the man telling it was my Prince Charming. There was no doubt he'd make all of it come true.

"I'm in for it, huh?" It was evil for me to pry, but I was evil.

"I'm going to take you up to our suite, or to our cabin, or where-the-fuck-ever, and I'm going to knock you up so hard."

I laughed from deep inside my belly. Laughing like that hurt, but it felt so, so good too.

He chided in a phony-as-hell serious Casey tone, "I'm serious. I'm putting babies right in you."

"Babies?" Plural? He is a twin.

Wait.

Twins are passed from the mother's side. Right? I'd have to research that. Before the epic impregnating anyway.

"Well, I'm going to do it all special-like. Wedding-sex style."

He held me close. My sides screamed, but I couldn't care less about the pain. My heart felt heavy with joy and love. That was one first I could give him. Actually, if I was counting, that was two. Wedding-sex and babies. I'd never had either.

"Hmm," I purred, pretending to consider it. I'd need to think about the babies. Well, a little. We'd at least need to have a permanent address decided, but lying there in his arms I was content to live the fantasy.

"What? What's all this hmm-ing? Where'd I lose ya?"

My head found the crook of his neck. He smelled so inviting. Like home.

"You didn't lose me."

"I hope I never do, honeybee."

We rested there that night curled up into one another and I thought—really thought—about vows. His arms wrapped around me. Both of our heads lying on one pillow. I'd be happy to be his to have and hold.

Forever.

TWO

Casey

Monday, June 14, 2010

THE LUXURY OF HAVING her there to hold all night was one I wouldn't take for granted. She *was* mine.

My Betty. My honeybee. My Blake.

I was hers. So fucking hers. I skated the thin line of being whipped. Whipped. What a joke. How many times had I given dudes shit for "being whipped?" I'd need to apologize, because whipped was the best place on earth. I bet Snapple was made in Whippedville.

It was those types of thoughts—the happy ones, the excited

ones—that diverted my otherwise livid mind.

She was home and safe and, most importantly, with me. Those were the other facts that quelled the rage I'd been feeling. Every wince. Every time she stared off into space. Every flinch. Every fucking time she said she didn't remember felt like a hammer to the side of my head. I saw red more in those quiet days than I ever had before. More than when she married the bastard. Even more than when she was in the hospital. Having her healthy and safe allowed my mind to wander.

That motherfucker would pay. I wasn't sure how, but he would. I'd told her about the fantasies I had of our future, but I didn't tell her any of the things I'd come up with to quench my thirst for revenge. Not even my revenge. It belonged to her.

I knew there was little I could do and that probably added to the helpless feeling of wanting justice I may never get. She claimed she couldn't remember, but I knew there were at least some things she did. I could read her.

It made me sick. It physically hurt thinking about that night.

Her sleeping, tear-stained face. The blood.

Holding in that kind of anger, for me—hell, for anyone—wasn't healthy, but I had to think about what was best for her. Blake not talking was much different than her lying about it. I understood her reasons.

I think everyone suspected there were details she was hiding, but she wasn't hiding them from us. It wasn't about us. She was shielding herself from that night until she was strong enough to sort through the details.

Her dad, her brothers, my family, they all felt like I did. It was a crazy way to get to know people, but that's what we had.

A common interest. *Her*.

Reggie and I were talking almost every day. He'd call to see how she was feeling and then the conversation would turn to what—if anything—was new in terms of *him*. That was another thing that changed. No one ever said *his* name. The reasons for that were most likely different for all of us, but for me it was one small way I could rid my life of *him*. I exterminated *him* from my vocabulary.

That motherfucking piece of shit.

She didn't have to remember. I have enough memories from that nightmare of a night for everyone.

Her lifeless limbs on the ground. Blood on the walls. Her lip busted.

I was there. I saw her. I'd tried my damnedest not to look, but I had. And Reggie saw her too. We shared that. Not the ideal way to bond with your soon-to-be brother-in-law, but again, that's what we had.

The moments where I felt relaxed, over that week, were few. I was terrified she'd need me and I'd be out cold. My body knew to stay half-awake. Admittedly, it caused my delirious mind to race even more.

However, after we talked about my plans, and I was able to clear my mind for the moment, I felt a little peace. She was asleep in front of me, her back against my chest, and there was nothing that could possibly happen to her.

I wouldn't let it.

There wouldn't be a *next* time she was treated like that. I'd rather die or rot in prison first.

So, as I should, I let my mind drift off while I was still

thinking about happier things. I concentrated on a perfect way to propose, and for the first time in over a week, I *almost* slept well.

"That sounds good, man," I said to Troy on the phone. "What time do you land?"

"About eleven. Want me to meet you at Bay? You can show me around."

I watched Blake fill up our coffee cups, the original Betty and Lou mugs from our first morning together. The words had long since faded, but the sentiment never would.

It was fairly early when Troy called. Hell, had he not reminded me, I would have forgotten he was coming into town to talk about a possible permanent position at the Seattle division of Bay Brewing I was opening. When he first seemed interested, I was slightly surprised. He had roots in San Francisco. Not deep ones, just lots of them. Bands. Other jobs. His mom was still floating around there somewhere, and for the most part, I thought it was strange he'd be willing to relocate so easily.

Whatever his reasons, I was happy he'd offered. He already knew a lot about Bay and how we did things. He'd fit right in and I trusted him. He didn't commit. Like ever. To anything. So having him say he was ready for something long-term struck me. He was serious.

"Hold on a second," I said, setting my hand over the receiver. I hadn't left Blake since the hospital, not for a second. The thought of it made me anxious, which I knew I'd need to get over. It just seemed so soon. She'd barely been home a week.

"Blake," I began and she cut me off.

"Go to work, Casey." Her smile said more than her words. It was genuine. I didn't know whether I liked or disliked that she wanted to get rid of me. If she wanted to be alone for a while, this would be a good start. I wasn't willing to travel back to San Francisco yet, not without her. I might never be. Besides, Audrey was right next door.

"Yes, ma'am," I said without resistance. If I was going to be a husband, it was a good time to take a lesson in picking my battles. I'd let her *think* she was winning that one. "Troy, want me to pick you up?"

"Nah, I need to rent a car. If everything goes well, I'll fly back in a week or so and drive my shit up. I need to look for a place to stay and get some shit lined up." He was already thinking about moving. That was a good sign. A great sign really. I wasn't sure how long we'd be in Seattle. It was a real possibility it would be forever. Comfort came from knowing I'd have my best friend close if I was away from most of my family. Everyone likes having a familiar face around.

When I finished the call with Troy, I heard Blake running water for a bath. I had the sneaky suspicion she was trying to seduce me. She thought she was ready. I was skeptical. I didn't want her doing anything that could hurt her healing body; so I needed to keep a watchful eye. When you have a girlfriend as hot as mine, *watching* was easy. Even banged-up and bruised, she was beautiful.

Now I had a few options. Succumb to the ornery flirt or walk away.

I knocked on the bathroom door. Fuck that walking-away shit. Those days were over. If I had it my way, we'd be officially living together. She was about to get a taste of what living with me would be like.

Of course, I respected her privacy, but I knew a couple of things about this girl. She knew I was leaving and if she wanted a private bath, she would have waited. And on top of that, she liked seeing me naked just as much.

"You can come in, Casey."

I was *so* on to her.

"I don't want to intrude," I chimed, playing the part of a red-feathered angel, knowing full well I wasn't going to give in to *everything* she wanted. Not yet. I wasn't sure if she was ready, and I sure as hell wasn't. The thought of hurting her was abhorrent to me. I could wait.

Barely.

I had to be sure she was all right, not just physically, but emotionally. She was good at pretending. That was a fact I'd learned a long time ago. She wasn't going to use me as an escape. Not at first anyway. She was going to deal with whatever battle she had going on inside. I hoped she would let me help. I desperately wanted to, about as bad as I wanted to be buried inside her.

"You're not. If you'd like, you can get in with me. There's room for both of us." She used her sing-song voice, and I prepared myself for a hell of a fight with my self-control. I turned the knob slowly, taking a few calming breaths. I hadn't ever spent so much time with her and *not*—well— been fucking. It would be a challenge not to take what I wanted. What I craved. Especially when she was so willing.

Upon opening the door, I found her leaning over the side of the big tub wearing a terrycloth robe. *A white terrycloth robe.* Exactly like the one she'd worn the first night we'd met. She wasn't fighting fair.

Hello, old friend.

"The water feels nice. Come here. I'll help you undress," she offered.

I changed my mind. Maybe I wouldn't take what I needed. Maybe I'd give. Or rather, let her take. You know what I mean. She'd gone to all this work and everything. She brought out the big guns. I'd basically just be there. Didn't have to ravage her the way my balls were begging me to. I didn't have to bend her over the counter and fuck her while I watched her come in front of me in the mirror. I could just be her tool. Her healing tool. A man can rationalize sex in about four seconds.

That notion had begun to grow on me. *Among other things.*

She wanted a diversion. And, hell if I couldn't sympathize with wanting to feel good. When I'd been at my lowest, her warm body, being there for mine, had never hurt. I'd just have to be careful.

Really careful.

"I'm going to say this quickly. Clearly you're taking hygiene to a whole new level, and who am I to stand in the way?" I asked as I took small measured steps near her. She sat on the edge of the tub and the loosely tied robe fell open a little more.

It was goddamn glorious. Her cleavage looked like a feast, and I was starving.

I had to focus, before I lost my train of thought.

I cleared my throat, because that's what you do when you're trying to jump-start words you're only half-ass sure about saying. "I know what you're doing."

Her head tipped downward, but I caught it.

Oh, honeybee. This isn't a rejection.

"Hear me out. I remember how devastated I felt when my mother passed away and how you were there for me. Granted, I didn't lure you in with soapy water and my A-game in sexual prowess, but I can't deny that you being there—being with me when I needed that connection—helped. I want to help you. I want to make you feel better and take all of it away. I can't though and doing this won't make any of it disappear. But maybe in some way it'll prove I'm here. I'm all in, honeybee." Damn it, she had to know, but I wasn't keen on guesswork anymore. Frankly, it was my pleasure having the opportunity to reassure her.

She needed it; so I needed to give it to her.

Her head fell to the side and she kissed my hand. I saw so much love in her eyes. It reduced my worry—if only for the moment—that she was still struggling.

"I do need you," she admitted as she stood. The robe fell away and she let it slip off her arms, never breaking eye contact. She spoke softly. "I want to feel a loving touch. I want to be swallowed whole by your goodness and tenderness. Casey, touch me so I know I'm not broken. I want this to be day one. I'm feeling better. I'm ready to start getting back to normal. Or at least start looking for our normal."

Those moments, where she let me see her vulnerability, seared her name on my heart. Being able to help the one you love most, makes you stronger. It never dawned on me that it wasn't the sex—a distraction, a high—but it wasn't. It was intimacy she was longing for.

She leaned into me and, if I needed any more convincing, she provided it. Her warm lips briefly met mine. Her timid, yet purposeful, hands began to undress me. They slipped under my T-shirt and ran over my stomach and around to my back as she lifted it off. Her fingers disappeared under the waist of my shorts and she pushed them down. Her breathing was controlled and deep.

I bent forward and pressed a kiss to her neck and a quiet moan filled the silence of the steamy bathroom as she moved to give me more of her skin. Her fingers laced with mine and she stepped into the bath. My arm around her waist insured she was steady.

For a brief moment, I took stock of the fading bruises on her body. Yellow and green cloud-like shapes painted all over her.

I swallowed emotion after emotion I felt.

She wanted a good day.

She wanted me.

I'd give her anything I could. I'd offer my body for us to share when hers needed mending. I'd touch her in a way that left no room for doubt that I'd always put her first. I couldn't heal her, but for the rest of my life I'd love her through sickness and health.

THREE

Blake

Monday, June 14, 2010

HE HEALED ME FROM the inside out. My pain turned to gentle pleasure.

"Love me," I begged.

"I do."

"Fix me."

"I will," he promised.

He gave me everything I craved that morning. Patiently, he watched me with hungry eyes. Never taking. Never rushing. For long minutes I slowly rose and fell over him. I enjoyed the sight of him beneath me, kissing my breasts. I savored every serene second. The sensation of our connection took over me, and it washed away some of the hurt, replacing agony with adoration.

"Make me yours."

"Honeybee, all of you belongs to me. Always has. These lips are mine. That bright pink nose. Your mistakes. Your smiles. This body. Your heart. Your future. All mine." His voice was thick with desire. He spoke words into my ears cloaked in love and unashamed possession, and I fell apart listening to him affirm how beautiful I was to him. He found his release as I held onto him for dear life.

Such simple passion, but as quiet as it was intense, it satisfied.

"I love you," he whispered tenderly as he stroked my back. The water had turned cold over time while I regained a little piece of myself. I was still straddling him and curled into his chest, having taken what I desired. It didn't feel like theft though, regardless of the robbery I'd staged. He offered himself freely without the objection I expected.

"We should get out of here before you sprout gills and fins," he said.

"I know. You need to get going." I was glad he was going to work. I could only speculate about the many things he'd pushed aside to care for me. Also, I knew he wouldn't leave if he was worried. I was getting better. I was healing on the outside enough that he trusted I'd be okay on my own for a while. I had to believe he was right.

"What are you going to do today?" He kissed my head as he stepped out of the bath.

"I don't know. I thought about going to the store. Maybe do some cooking. What sounds good for dinner?"

What sounds good for dinner? Was this real?

As I took the towel he offered, I could see that the silly, mundane question excited him too. I never wanted to take these small things for granted.

"Kiss me," he requested with puckered lips.

A tiny milestone and a turn in the most precious of directions. I was so damn lucky I'd get to have conversations like this—with him—for the rest of our lives. Well, if he ever asked me to marry him.

Shit. Did the paperwork even matter?

I gave him a quick kiss in exchange for the towel he'd already finished using and bent to wrap it around my head. My side still ached, but it was improving. I stood up and watched as he prepared to shave in front of the mirror.

"What can you make?"

"Please," I scoffed. "Name it. I can make it."

"I want ribs." He swathed the fluffy foam over his face, then wiped and methodically cleared a stripe from his lips with the back of his thumb. Even with a snow-white Barbasol beard he was the sexiest thing I'd ever seen.

"Ribs are doable. Hey, if you want, ask Troy if he wants to come over."

He nodded as he ran the razor down his cheek and along his outstretched neck, then tapped it clean in the warm water pooled in the sink. He winked at me when he caught me staring at his reflection from behind him, and said, "You need to call Reggie. He called after you fell asleep on the couch last night."

"I will." I'd do whatever he said if he winked at me like that. That tiny gesture affirming everything was going to be all right. *I love that man and his wink.*

I kissed his shoulder and left him to it.

After reminding me he was just a phone call away no less than three times and kissing me goodbye twice and finally pulling away, I made a list of things I needed around the house and the items I'd need for dinner.

It had been nice having people take care of me—well, kind of—but I was in need of human-sustaining items, and my little apartment—not accustomed to so many people coming in and out—was showing a real need of cleaning. It wasn't a mess, but it wasn't in order. *My* order anyway. I didn't have OCD, and I certainly wasn't a clean freak, but—like most people—my things needed to be the way I liked them.

They'd all done a good job of making sure the trash was out and the dishes were done, but things weren't in their typical places. Coffee mugs were in the wrong cabinet. My refrigerator looked weird. Call me crazy, but condiments belong in the door of a refrigerator, not the shelves. Silverware handles should all be going the same direction in the drawers. The toilet paper should be under the sink and not simply in an open pack next to the toilet. It was small tweaks like that which begged for my attention. None of them truly mattered, but when you're trying to feel normal, having your house feel like *your* space is essential. So I swept through my place and took pleasure in making it feel like mine again.

Before the hospital, I'd never had so many people in my space. Audrey would come by every few days for a glass of wine—which she wasn't quite old enough for yet—but she lived right next door. And Casey came to visit a couple of times, but mostly I'd been going to California on weekends.

It dawned on me that my small apartment was actually feeling like a home. A very tiny one at least. Then it made me miss Casey's house. That place was a home. Thoughts of living there were becoming commonplace, and if that's where he wanted to be, regardless of having bought a brewery here in Seattle, I'd go willingly. Shit. I might even suggest it.

It was comforting to me that I would be where he was. We'd park in the same driveway. Have all the same keys. He might even fill up my gas tank, if I was lucky. We'd share duties and chores and trivial tasks, which in the moment, didn't seem trivial at all. They were exactly what we'd been fighting for.

It invigorated me, and I was as happy as a clam while I cleaned.

Straightening up my room, I found a pile of Casey's clothes by his duffel bag. Absentmindedly, I cleaned out a drawer in my dresser for him. He shouldn't have to live out of a bag. Not anymore. He wasn't a visitor. He wasn't a guest. He was permanent. I knew that to my core. I stashed away his underwear and socks in a small drawer and then emptied another for his undershirts and shorts. I hung up the shirts that seemed clean, having still been folded in his bag.

It was funny how little men packed. His toiletries were already in my bathroom, out on the sink, so I gave them real estate in my cabinet.

When all was where it belonged, I collected his and my dirty clothes to wash. I won't say it was my wildest dream to do his dirty laundry, but the thought of taking care of him bloomed a weird sort of hope in me. As I walked to the machines, I smelled one of his worn shirts. His singularly-Casey scent filled my lungs.

Was it creepy? Probably.

Did I care? Not a bit.

That reminded me, Casey had been using shampoo to wash with. I smiled knowing I'd buy him bath wash and anything else he needed. So when equilibrium was returned to the small apartment, I sat at the breakfast bar and made a list of household things we needed. Coffee. I needed real beans. The already-ground stuff had been serving its purpose, but I desperately craved the taste of a freshly ground cup of joe. Deodorant. Paper towels. He needed more razors. It lit me up inside that my grocery list consisted of things for him.

Fact. I'd been married, but I'd never even thought of doing those sorts of things for Grant. I never worried about his razor being dull or if he preferred a certain laundry soap.

I wondered if there would ever be a time when I didn't compare my relationship with Casey to the one I thought I had with Grant. Before the wedding, before everything came out, there wasn't a time I could remember when being domestic with *him*—for him—seemed appealing. It never even occurred to me to do his laundry. I'd never thought about what he'd like for dinner. There was never a *we* in that marriage. No *us* to speak of.

If there were a pill I could take to make him disappear from my memory, I'd take two, just in case. My ambivalence to him had changed. Intensified. I didn't just not want him; I *hated* him.

I consciously made myself push him to the back of my

memory. He only existed if I let him. As soon as the reminders were physically gone from my body, and my name changed—back to Warren, and to Moore—he'd be gone.

He was my biggest mistake.

I shook my head. My hands clenched the edge of the counter as I, one-by-one, collected the vile thoughts of Grant and put them in a box. Then I imagined locking it and mailing the key to the Arctic.

Don't let him ruin today.

House clean. Laundry going. I kept moving forward.

I chatted with Micah on the phone for a while before I decided to knock on Audrey's door and see if she wanted to join us for dinner.

"Hey you," she said cheerily. "How are you feeling? You look so much better."

I accepted her compliment and let it fuel my need to *be* better.

"I'm feeling human again, so that's a start."

She laughed and turned, leaving the door open, and silently inviting me in. There was music playing, but I didn't recognize the band.

"Ignore my mess," she said as she tried to tidy the table covered in modeling clay and tools. "I've been up all night working on something." She didn't look like she'd been up all night. Her hair was recently washed and she looked fresh as a damn daisy. Here I'd gotten the best sleep I'd had in over a week and I still looked like a zombie.

"I won't keep you. I just wanted to see what you were doing for dinner," I mentioned as I studied the piece she was constructing. It was a heart. Anatomically correct, from what I could tell. "I'm cooking."

"You are?"

"Yeah, I need to do something. I'm going stir crazy. I talked to my boss yesterday, but he told me to take the rest of the week off. So, I thought I'd grill and we could chill out back. It's not supposed to rain so we might as well take advantage." Before I spent so much time in San Francisco, I'd never really noticed the rain in Seattle, but now it drove me nuts.

"Yeah, sure. That sounds great. I could use some real food."

"Cool. Troy is in town so Casey's going to see if he wants to come over too."

Audrey took a deep breath and paused, holding what looked like one of those tools a dentist uses.

"I might just swing by for a bit. I—I'm kind of into this thing I'm working on. If you can't tell," she added and nervously laughed. The normally cool and easy-breezy Audrey suddenly looked uncomfortable.

"What's wrong? You get along with Troy, don't you?" That was the only thing I could think of that would make her demeanor change so quickly. She'd been over almost every night when we ordered food in. From what Casey had said in the past, Troy was basically their third brother. Why would him being there change anything?

"Nothing's wrong. I just want to get this finished is all. I might show it at a friend's gallery, if I get it done before the next exhibition. I'm not that great with clay, and it's really driving me crazy. And I'm just tired." She smiled, but it was weak.

If there was one thing I knew, it was a lie like that. Over the past few years I'd become an expert at hiding the real truth with legit excuses. But, if she didn't want to talk about it, I wasn't going to pry—yet. I knew what it's like to feel cornered.

"That's fine. We'll be out back later. I'll text you when the food's ready. I'm running out to the store in a bit. Need anything?"

"Nah, I'm fine. I just went yesterday." She sat down at the chair in front of her sculpture and began scrutinizing, turning it on the spinning platform she'd built it on.

"Okay, well just text if you think of anything," I said as I walked back to the door. "I'll see you later."

"Yeah, okay."

I wondered if Casey knew why she'd acted so odd. Had I missed something while I was down and out?

Me: Have you talked to Audrey?

Casey: Not today. Are you all right?

Me: I'm fine. She just seemed a little strange.

Casey: She IS a little strange.

Me: You're funny. How's it going? Troy make it in?

Casey: Yep. He's already running the place and I haven't even hired him yet. What are you doing?

Me: Going to the store. Doing laundry.

Casey: Don't overdo it. I can go to the store if you tell me what we need.

I thought about telling him I needed tampons and other unmentionables, but decided to go easy on him. Then I smiled knowing there would come a time when I'd thoroughly enjoy seeing his reaction to such requests. He'd undoubtedly say yes, but I'd want to see his face.

Me: I won't overdo anything. I feel fine.

Casey: Did you call your brother?

Man. Those two were a pair. It was a double-edged sword having my brother, Reggie, and Casey becoming friends. Since Reggie returned to Chicago last week, they were in—what seemed like—constant communication. I'd call him, but I could just about predict the whole conversation.

He'd ask how I was feeling. I'd ask if he'd talked to Nora lately. I'd say fine; he'd say no. He'd ask me if I'd remembered anything about that night—again. Same as every time we spoke.

It wasn't that I didn't want to talk to Reggie. I wasn't intentionally avoiding him—okay, I was. I didn't want to talk about *it*. That night. And he was relentless. I might be a practiced liar, but I was never good at it. Changing the subject and saying things were still fuzzy wasn't going to last long with him.

Just like when he witnessed Casey and me at the airport and made me spill my guts, he wouldn't give up until he knew.

Me: I'm about to.

Casey: Good. He's cool and all, but that dude can be scary.

Me: Please. He's harmless.

I grinned at my phone. I was a lucky girl to have so many people who cared about me. It was a small thing, but if my calling gave them peace of mind, it was the least I could

Before my eyes, my family was naturally becoming
Or, rather, our two families were blending into one. Just like a
we and an *us* should.

FOUR

Reggie

Monday, June 14, 2010

"YEAH, SHE'S DOING CONSIDERABLY better. Thanks for asking," I assured Nora from behind my desk. Calling her from the waiting room in the hospital last week had been a weak moment. We hadn't spoken much over the past year, until that night. Now she was calling almost every day to see how my little sister was doing. The sound of her voice was calming, and in those minutes, the repetitive chatter inside my head muted. She'd always had that effect on me.

Clarity.

"Good, so how are *you*?" she asked.

That was a loaded fucking question.

How was I?

I was focused. I was driven. I wasn't about to let myself fall back into the fantasy that I could have it all, because I couldn't. We both knew how this would end. If you could even call it an end. It never really began. Unless you call a few hot nights with a woman who doesn't understand the concept of monogamy, the beginning of anything—other than a huge pain in the ass.

That wasn't totally fair. We had a friendship too, but that wasn't enough. Not for me.

"You know me. I'm good." What I wanted to ask her was *how is whoever* they *are keeping your bed warm at night?* But I knew it wasn't worth the effort asking for two reasons: She wouldn't tell me, and she never let anyone stay long enough for the sheets to get warm.

"Well, I'm glad everything is working out. They've had a rough road."

I must have missed that it was Understatement Day on my calendar. The messed-up part was even though we were only making small talk, only approaching un-touchy subjects, it made me feel better knowing she was there. *Still.* After all this time. I may never know completely what her feelings for me were, but it was undeniable she had them. It was a huge fucking shame we could never agree about certain fundamental ideas on relationships.

Like I wanted her to be mine and she didn't understand the concept.

My phone beeped indicating I had another call coming in. *Blake.* Of all the times for her to call me back, she picked now.

Lovely.

"Listen, are you going to be around for a little while?" I stood and looked out into the city. From the fifty-fifth floor I could see everything.

"What's a little while?"

"Ten minutes? My sister's calling," I replied, trying my damnedest not to be compulsive. Not to count. Not to *tell* her to wait.

"I don't know."

"I'll call you back in ten minutes, Nora. If you can't talk, don't answer. It's that simple." I hated speaking to her like that. I missed the times when things were easier. When we'd chat on the phone, or have dinner, or share a drink after work … before the arbitrary lines she'd drawn had been crossed.

"Bye, Reggie." She hung up. She never was one for fighting back. Why would she? Bottom line: she didn't need me.

"Hello," I answered with a bit of forced cheerfulness as I switched lines.

"Hello to you," Blake said.

She sounded infinitely better than she had on Saturday. I had no doubt in my mind Casey was taking care of her. Watching him go through hell, like the rest of us, waiting for her to wake up in the hospital, only proved one thing. He loved the fuck out of her. And, beyond that, I knew the rest was just semantics.

"How are you doing today?"

"Better. I'm about to go to the store."

That was a pleasant surprise. I never wanted to see her the way we'd found her that night again. Beaten. Battered. Broken.

"By yourself?"

"Yeah, all by myself. I'm driving a car, and I even have my own money." And there was her sarcasm. She was back to being a little shit again. The return of her gusto was welcome.

She'd changed a lot since the beginning of the year, and seeing some of that fight return was definitely a great thing. It was especially good, because I had some news she probably wasn't going to like. She'd need that fight.

"Well, before you head out, we need to talk."

I looked at my watch. *Eight minutes to call Nora.*

"About what, Reggie? I've told you I can't really remember anything," she recited for exactly the thirtieth time in the past week.

I stopped her before she could finish. "I didn't want to say anything to Casey, but you know my friend Paul, the cop?"

"Yeah."

"He called me yesterday. He heard at the station that Grant changed his story. Since he's looking at a pretty steep fine, probably even a little jail time for the stunt with the gun, he's looking for a way out. Paul says Grant's claiming Casey did that to you and that's why he had his gun drawn. To protect himself and *you*."

"No. That's not true," she snapped, almost shouting.

"I know it's not true, because I rode over there with Casey. I told Paul that, but Blake, if you can't remember, it's just his word against ours. He's saying it to get himself out of trouble. If they have a reason to believe he was acting in self-defense, they might drop some of the charges."

"He can't do that. Casey didn't hurt me. Grant did."

Now we were getting somewhere. She'd never said that out loud to me. Sure I wanted Blake to open up about it, but I never wanted it to be like this. I never wanted her to feel forced—or cornered—by Grant to do *anything* ever again, but this was the game he was playing. For all he knew, she couldn't remember and he saw it as a way out. And a way to cause some shit for Casey in the process. I imagined, in the end, it would eventually go to trial or he'd take a plea with a lesser charge.

"That's not right, Reggie." The panic in her voice was unmistakable. "That's not true. He can't do that. Why can't he just leave me alone?"

"Blake, are you sure you can't remember?"

There was a pause. A long pause. A truth-confessing pause.

I had three minutes to call Nora. Why did I say only ten minutes?

"Hey, don't stress out about it right now. Okay? Paul said Grant made his statement and asked if I could come in to make mine and answer a few more questions. I'll be in town on Thursday."

"What will they do to Casey?"

"They'll probably call him to come in too, or they might even arrest him. I wanted to give you guys a heads-up. Paul said it would just be a formality, but it'd most likely happen in the next few days. Loverboy might want to call his lawyer, just so they're ready. I thought maybe you'd want to tell him yourself." It was a bad position to be in, especially since I *knew* she remembered some, if not all that had happened. Even I could tell, and I'd only seen her twice since she'd woken up, right before I came back to Chicago, but I'd talked to her on the phone plenty. It was in her voice. My money was to bet on her assuming Grant was in enough trouble—even without her statement or her pressing any charges—and she simply wanted to be done with him.

"That's … that's so wrong though." Sheer terror echoed in her voice.

I hated that motherfucker for what he did to her. I didn't know Casey all that well yet, but I kind of hated Grant for him too. The Casey I was quickly getting to know wouldn't put up with his shit though. And despite her efforts, I didn't think she was afraid of Casey going to jail. She knew what happened. She wouldn't let Grant do anything to him. She was just scared of letting it all out.

That's the way my little sister operated. Always had been. One time when we were kids she ripped the shit out of the bottom of her foot. It got infected, but the little shit wouldn't tell anyone until it started making her sick. That girl could hold things in like no one else I knew, but she had her tells.

"Don't worry, Blake. Casey will be all right."

"I know he will," she said. In the span of two minutes she'd changed her tune. She didn't sound like a victim, and that was exactly what I wanted. She'd just gotten there a lot faster than I predicted.

"If you know anything, it's probably a good time to talk to someone. Even if it is just Casey." I hoped I wasn't overestimating his control—his ability to stay calm. I also hoped that when she called him, he'd handle it with wisdom and *not* with emotion.

I didn't know though.

Part of me thought he'd be more wrapped up in making sure she was okay. The other part worried if he heard the words we both knew were true come out of her mouth, he might snap. Fuck. I'd like to think I'd be wise and smart about it too, but Heaven only knows the reach of *my* control.

"I know," she admitted with a new edge to her voice. I had to hand it to her. She was tougher than any of us ever gave her credit for. "Reggie? Speaking of talking to someone, have you talked to Nora lately?"

And she was a goddamned expert at turning shit around.

"No."

Fuck. Ten minutes. I was breaking my own rule.

"Blake, tell Casey to call me if he wants to know anything. I can give him Paul's number if he has any questions. I have to go. I love you."

Eleven minutes.

"I will. Thanks for letting me know. I love you too. Bye," she said before the line went dead.

I'd said ten minutes. I never told half-truths. I believed in all or nothing, but my finger scrolled to her number anyway.

Fuck my rules.

"Well, well. That was longer than *ten* minutes. Did you lose track of time?"

Wasn't she coy? Her voice was covered in sarcasm knowing that it was eating me up to be late.

"Well, it was either not call and possibly miss you while you're in town—or call."

"Look at you meeting me halfway." Why wouldn't she do the same?

"That's not what this is and you know it." The women in my life never went easy on me.

"Our place?" she asked.

"Ten minutes."

"Don't be late this time." Then she hung up and there was no chance in hell I'd be late twice.

FIVE

Casey

Monday, June 14, 2010

"ALL RIGHT, MAN. WHAT do you think of the place?"

The new Bay Brewing satellite branch was still a ways out from up and running, but it had the promise of being a great location. The building was in a thriving part of town and the fucker was huge. The equipment it could hold was awesome. Since we'd just expanded the San Fran branch into a neighboring building, we were getting the kettles and other brewing machinery from the same manufacturer we'd used before. For now, we had a few guys from California cleaning the empty space to prepare for the large equipment.

There was a lot to be done, but we'd get there.

"It's great," he said, wide eyes looking around. The big brick building was impressive, and since there was nothing inside, it seemed to go on and on.

"We've talked about putting in a small bar/retail area and having tours here in the future."

"Yeah, you've got the space for it." He chuckled. "Shit. You're really doing it, dude. This is great."

"Where's your poker face? You're supposed to make me beg you to work for me."

"Nah, I'm in. I've been wanting something a little more stable and what you've done—I can't say I'm not a little jealous."

Pride swelled in my chest. I'd worked hard and this was the result. It wasn't mine alone, but I owned my fair share. Troy would be a solid, permanent addition.

"So what are you thinking? Sales, management, shipping and receiving? What are you interested in doing here?" It was time to cut the shit and find out what he was into. I wasn't a manager by nature, but it wasn't that different from sales. Give someone what they want and they'll be happy. Happy workers make happy beer. Or some shit like that.

"I don't want to travel like you do. I'm ready to work nine-to-five, Casey. You know how I grew up. I'm ready to put my roots down. But *management*?" He was skeptical.

"Yeah, *management*. I'm not a fool. This isn't some 'Hey, let my bro run my shit into the ground' kind of thing. I trust you. I know you'll call me if you need something, but mostly I need someone to be here when I'm not. Make sure orders are entered. Make sure trucks leave full and get where they're going. Keep the peace." And as much as it sounded like bullshit, anyone who could manage having six different jobs at the same time for as long as he did—well, fuck if that wasn't qualification enough. I needed a juggler and one that everyone would like.

"You'll be the ground control; I'll be Major Tom. I'm not throwing you to the sharks, Troy."

I'd known him my whole life and I could trust the guy with anything. That was something you couldn't interview for. He could do it. He was ready.

"I'm here for whatever you need," he confirmed with a nod, letting it all sink in. I doubted anyone had ever just handed him responsibility like that. I was excited to see what he'd do with it. A shit-eating grin spread across his face. "So, let's talk dollars."

I laughed. "I'll get you drunk, and then we'll talk numbers."

We'd walked through the whole facility and ended on the docks where Rhett and Eric, up from San Francisco, were taking a break.

"You guys have gotten a lot done in the last week," I commented, giving Rhett a quick handshake.

"Yeah, well you've been out of our hair," he joked.

The original plan was I'd be here helping. Pulling out remnants of the last occupant and getting it up to food and beverage standards for our permits and licenses.

That had all changed on a dime, but they didn't let that slow them down. "Sorry about that, guys."

Eric scoffed. "Don't worry about it. How's everything going? She feeling better?"

They didn't know everything, but I'd worked with them in some capacity for the past six years. I wasn't sure what Marc told them, and it didn't bother me that they knew *some* of the situation.

"A little better every day," I said. "Thanks for asking."

Troy gave me a knowing look, but I left it at that.

"So what do you think, Troy? You ready to do this?" Rhett asked. The six-foot-tall ginger had pretty much the same job at the home branch as I'd just offered Troy. I'm sure one of them would have taken the job, but the move would be much easier for someone who was willing to pick up and relocate to a city where they only knew two people. Well three, if you counted Audrey.

Only then had it dawned on me. He'd be here to look out for her when we weren't. The situation just got better and better.

It was shaping up to be a good fucking day.

"You guys have a lot more to do today?" I asked them. "We'll help you finish up and then you guys can come with us for a few cold ones." I owed them. What they'd accomplished in the last week was a huge fucking job for three grown men, and they'd done just about all of it with only two.

"Not much. We're just waiting on a truck bringing some shit we need to get this place clean. Then we're good for the day," Rhett said with a thirsty grin.

"What time are you guys starting in the morning?" Troy inquired.

By the look on Eric's face, he was impressed Troy would step up so fast. He answered, "Probably about six. You coming?"

"Damn right. Sooner we get this place running, the better."

"Day one and already improving productivity," I cracked.

It was great to catch up with some men. Like dudes, you know? Men who had their shit together, and were just living life day-by-day. We had some good guys on our team and everyone had great stuff going on. Things I'd never considered. Starting a family. Making a home.

As beers flowed at a pub only a few blocks from the new Bay location, we shot the shit. Eric had a ton of kids and one on the way. He texted his wife nothing short of three times from the bar to check up on her. Rhett had just bought a house and he was talking about the demo project he was doing.

Hearing how happy these guys were made me eager to get started on *our* life. Mine and Blake's.

Troy listened, interested, and I could see some of those things appealed to him, just like they did me.

"So you gonna put a ring on that girl's finger, Casey?" Eric asked.

"Fucking right I am. I've been waiting a long time to make her mine and the time is up." I laughed, but then thought—a *ring.* I needed to work on that. I'd need major help. I didn't know jack-shit about jewelry.

"He's been hot after that girl for years," Troy told them.

Then he insisted on telling them how I was wrapped around her finger from the word go and how I'd rigged meeting up with her at trade shows.

He was cracking them up. The way he told the story was far different from how it had felt at times, but it gave me a chance to shoot a quick text to Reggie.

Me: What's your mom's number?

It took him a few minutes to reply.

Reggie: Why? What's wrong? Should I be worried?

Me: No. Nothing like that. I need her help.

He sent her number, and then followed it up with a message that was evidence the Warren sense of humor was hereditary.

Reggie: My dad will kick your ass if you put the move on his woman. He already told me he had an eye on you.

Their dad didn't have anything to worry about. I had eyes for one woman, and one alone.

Me: LOL He told me that too.

I'd call her mom on the way back to the apartment to see if she could meet me sometime that week and help me find a ring. Honeybee wasn't going to wait long, and I didn't want her to.

After an hour or so, Eric and Rhett said they needed to go. They were catching a ball game that night. I was thankful because, even though I knew she was okay, I was ready to get back to my girl.

The thing that surprised me most about the past week, being with her night and day? It still wasn't enough. I'd never tire of seeing or talking to her. Taking out the trash, or having meals together. Even though I'd fallen in love with her, never getting to experience so many firsts, each day felt like it was full of them now.

Since I'd only had two beers, I offered to drive. I told Troy we'd pick up the rental car the next day. I didn't think Blake would mind, but I kind of offered her small spare room to him—at least for the night. Besides, he mentioned he was eager to find a place of his own.

If Blake moves in with me, he could have her place.

Thoughts like that ran wild through my mind. Was there such a thing as too fast for us anymore? Not to me.

"Honeybee, I'm home," I sang as we walked through the front door. No knocking. No waiting for her to let me in. Our spaces were already becoming shared. Naturally. Oh, and I had a key.

She'd kept the door locked, which made me think too much.

Was she afraid?

Did she always do that?

Would he come here?

I shook off the curveball thoughts my mind threw at me and, instead of treading through bullshit, chose to find my girl and get my fucking lips some satisfaction. It had only been a few hours, but those demanding fuckers needed what they needed.

"Hi," she greeted me with a smile from the kitchen. She was busy in her element. "Hey, Troy. How'd you like the new building?"

"It's damn big, but it'll fill up fast. How are you feeling?" he asked, walking around the counter to give her a hug. He was gentle, knowing what she'd been through.

When she gave him a kiss on the cheek, he teased, "Oh, keep going. Casey. Dude. Fuck off. We need a minute. She needs to see what a real man is like." He pretended like he was ravaging her neck and she laughed easily as he playfully nuzzled her.

I felt no jealousy. None. In fact, I liked seeing how well she fit into my life and how my people loved her as much as I did. Her presence wasn't through telling my friends and family about her, finally they saw her magic firsthand. Of course they loved her like I did; she was magnificent.

And when it came to her laughs, in those days, I wasn't picky. I'd take hearing her giggle, no matter where it came from or who was making her happy. Watching her come back to life was something I wouldn't take for granted.

"I'm feeling good. You were right though," she said to me, waving him away. "I'm getting a little worn out." She chuckled and fanned herself, conceding to what I'd told her earlier.

"Well, I'm here now. Put me to work, Chef." There were ribs marinating in something that smelled smoky and sweet. She'd made guacamole and a pasta salad. On a separate platter there were vegetables skewered and seasoned, prepped for the grill.

"It's all ready to go. I'm just waiting for it to heat up and then the ribs can go on."

I opened the refrigerator to grab three beers for us as Troy carried the trays outside for Blake. She'd found Bay beer somewhere.

God, I fucking loved her.

It was the perfect time of night. The sun was behind the

trees giving the small backyard shade as we cooked and talked about Seattle and music and normal things. There was nothing spoken about beatings or divorces or dicks who needed to be shot.

"So where's Audrey?" Troy asked.

My arms were wrapped around Blake's waist as she checked the ribs one last time. They smelled like fucking heaven.

Blake answered, "I said I'd send her a message when the food was done. She's working on this incredible sculpture thing."

To that he replied, "That smells about done. Oh hell, I'll go get her." He jumped up from his seat at the patio table. "Besides, you two are ruining my appetite."

I waited until I heard the door shut and Blake had the last rib on the platter before I turned her around in my arms and took a few steps away from the heat of the grill.

"Hear that? We're making people sick," I said conspiratorially.

Her pretty brown eyes lit up. The past week's medication haze had cleared. They were brighter. More focused and all on me.

"What a shame," she teased, playing along.

"Fuck 'em. I've waited too fucking long for the days when I could put my hands on you whenever I wanted. There ain't no stopping me now." There never would be again. I was joking and messing around, but the undertone was still there. I think we were both getting used to being open about how we felt around others. We'd trained ourselves to starve when everyone around us feasted on love. It was our time to binge.

My hands found her cheeks, and I held her face still as I took my time looking at her. The swelling and bruising was nearly gone and the cut on her lip was healing. She leaned into me for a kiss and before our mouths met she murmured, “I love you.”

She tasted like forever.

SIX

Audrey

Monday, June 14, 2010

O*H MY GOD. MY stomach.*

I was hungry and smelling the barbeque floating through my open windows didn't help. Familiar aromas and faint sounds swam through my apartment. I knew he was close.

I sat at my table, same as I had all day. Not working on the heart, just looking at it. I'd been there for hours. Examining the piece. Scrutinizing it. Looking for what was missing. There were two hearts at my table and neither mine nor the one made of the expensive polymer clay had what they needed.

Depth.

Emotion.

Love.

Most of my art flourished out of feelings, but this piece was different. When I began, I thought it was my heart, but it wasn't. It was his. As the concept took shape in my head, I realized it was a heart I could never reach. One I'd never quite touch. One that not many ever would.

A heart under glass with a hand touching the clear plate on the other side.

It wasn't my typical venture. Most of my pieces were paintings or photographs I'd manipulated to show one underlying theme. One idea. One emotion.

This was going to be different, because it was so many emotions I'd lost count.

My hands lay where they had for hours, side by side on the wooden table top. Patiently waiting for direction. But I didn't have any.

I knew the vision. I could see it clearly, but something was stopping me from creating it.

A lot like his presence, his words always had a way of making me second-guess myself. My feelings. What I wanted.

You're a brat, Audrey. You're a kid, Audrey. You're their sister, Audrey.

I didn't care.

You're not that much older. I'm going away to school. It's none of their business.

I knew it was a dangerous path to let my mind walk, reliving those conversations. Because soon the words always led back to one memory. One night. One encounter where we didn't have ages and nothing else mattered.

I let him pull my hair as he took what he'd sworn all along he was protecting. My innocence. Only I'd lied that night and said I didn't have any. That it'd been taken long before then.

It was the only memory I have of us where he didn't hold back.

At the time, I didn't have anything to compare it to. I didn't know what was normal or how I should feel.

Lost in my thoughts, I didn't hear him come in until he said, "Wow, kid. Look at all of these. You're getting really good. Far better than the stick figure pictures you used to draw for me."

For as far back as I could remember I hung on his every word. Now his words hung themselves in me like priceless paintings on the inside of my chest.

"Don't you know how to knock?"

"Don't you know how to lock your door?" he retorted light-heartedly.

His hair was a little shorter in the back, but still long enough on top to fall perfectly around his face as he looked down at his boots, grinning like the devil. He loved playing with me.

"Is that what you came over here to tell me?"

"No. I came over here to tell you I'm moving to town."

"This town is pretty big. I'm sure we can find our own space." I considered throwing some of the sharp words he'd wounded me with time after time, but I didn't have it in me. He'd know I was just being a bitch. Or childish. Or delusional. Because they'd never be true out of my mouth.

He cocked his head to the side and gave me a look that begged for me to drop the act.

So I mocked him and gave it back.

The distance between us closed; my turncoat body reacted to him.

"Cut the shit, kid. You know why I moved here."

Did I?

Casey told me he was getting a job at the brewery, and Troy probably needed a new crop of women to fuck. My best estimates were that he'd been with most of the available ladies in San Francisco, and probably a few more who weren't.

"Troy, I'm here going to school. I'm in college. I'm experimenting and living my life. Just like you told me to do." Some of that was true. I'd been with a few guys, but no one who made any lasting impressions. "Welcome to Seattle. But I'm not the little sweet, forbidden kid-sister anymore. Not here."

"That's what I was counting on."

Then his brazen hand was in the nape of my hair, my pounding chest was crushed against his and our lips went to war.

SEVEN

Blake

Monday, June 14, 2010

CASEY TASTED LIKE THE only thing that would ever satisfy me completely. I savored everything about that kiss.

Earlier I'd spoken to Dr. Rex, and told her pretty much everything over the phone in a rush to confide in someone, in the event that the police were faster than Reggie thought they'd be. She'd know the story. She'd know the truth before I had a real reason to lie about it. Not that I was lying anymore, but if Grant tried to twist it around, I'd have someone on our side. Someone credible.

She'd said, just like I thought she would, "Tell Casey. Blake, you'll feel better. Tell him everything. There's no need to worry, sweetheart." I agreed. What Reggie told me knocked me off balance a little. I'd figured Grant would try something, do something, continue to cause trouble. But did he really have a leg to stand on?

The thought of the attack going to trial made my stomach queasy as I cooked that afternoon. But that's one of the things I loved most about cooking. I could do it while my mind was somewhere else. I could cut and chop my frustrations out. So I did.

We'd have a nice dinner. Spend time with Troy and Audrey, if she wasn't too busy. Then when everything settled down for the night, I'd talk to him.

Even though we weren't miles apart anymore, and we could call or text at any time of the day we pleased, I noticed it was at night when we still communicated best. When everything was quiet. When everything was set-aside until the next day. The same as we'd done by phone—where we talked about things we'd done when we were young, or what we'd done that day—those precious minutes were ours alone.

That's when I'd tell him about that night.

As he kissed me, both of us barefoot in the grass, I knew it was time to do it. I wasn't going to let Grant, or my own fear, ruin anything I was blessed enough to have now. And if I'd learned anything, it was that the truth hurt, but it healed you faster.

"I love you back, honeybee. So you're feeling worn out?"

he asked as he moved my hair behind my ears.

"A little."

His eyebrows rose, challenging me to tell the whole truth. When he made that face, and his forehead wrinkled, he wasn't one to toy with. The look said both: out with it, and I'll get it out of you anyway.

"Okay, I'm beat. My back hurts. My ribs hurt. And my scalp is itching like crazy. I can't wait to get these stitches out tomorrow." It had been longer than the suggested ten days, but I'd been feeling so tired last week that I'd made the appointment for after the weekend.

"That's better. I'll get the plates and stuff while you take a seat."

Audrey came through the wooden door that adjoined our two small yards just then. She looked almost angry, but when she saw Casey and me, she softened. She was working really hard on that project and Troy, just showing up, probably pissed her off. She was always particular about her art. There'd been times when she hadn't let me see something she was working on until it was completely finished, so having it right there in the open for everyone must have been like having your guts spilled out for the public's appraisal.

"You look like you mean business," Casey noted as he passed her on his way in to get plates and silverware.

"Don't forget paper towels. Just bring the roll," I shouted behind him.

"This smells really good, Blake. I'm starving." I doubted she'd eaten all day.

"Thanks. So how's it going over there? Getting close?" I

took a seat at the table and she followed bringing the trays from the grill.

"I just smashed it," she said in a huff. Then she picked a spare rib off the platter and began eating it. She tore into it like she was inflicting pain on the poor piece of barbecue.

"Smashed it?" I asked in shock. The heart she'd molded looked like it was all but finished when I'd seen it earlier. How could she just destroy it?

"Yep. It wasn't working. Some hearts just don't work the way they should," she scoffed between hungry bites. I wondered if she was talking about more than just the clay heart.

Casey and Troy came out with what we needed and everyone dug in, so I didn't get to ask any more about the piece. I could always ask her tomorrow when it was a little quieter.

We ate the meat like savages. I don't mean to sound like a braggart, but it was perfect. Listening to their moans of appreciation proved it. Or else they were just doing that to make me feel good. Didn't matter, because as banged up and bruised and nervous as I was about the conversation we'd be having—I did feel good. Better than I'd felt in a very, very long time.

"Anyone need another beer while I'm up?" Troy asked when we were piling up the remnants of the meal.

"I'm good," Casey chimed.

"I'm fine, thanks," I said.

Then Audrey said confidently, without hesitation, "I'll take one." The look on Casey's face was priceless. He was both shocked and torn. I could imagine the idea of his little sister drinking, bouncing around in his sexy mind. She hadn't asked for his permission, and I wasn't sure if he'd give it. He just shook his head like he couldn't believe it. Hell, he probably drank at a much younger age than she was.

"Audrey, I'm so proud that your first beer will be one of mine, because I'm sure my sweet, innocent little sister doesn't drink." Big brother sarcasm at its finest.

"Right," she said with all of the ambivalence of a nineteen-year-old. "I hope I like it."

"For the first time in my life, I hope someone doesn't love my beer," Casey muttered under his breath as he snatched up the last few dirty paper towels on the table.

The warm sun sinking out of sight told me it was only late in the evening, but I knew I wouldn't last long. I didn't want to tear Casey away from his friend or his sister, but what I needed to do was weighing heavily on my mind and it couldn't wait much longer.

He must have sensed my energy running low, because before I could say anything, he announced, "I hate to cut the evening short, but I've got a lot to do tomorrow, and I think this one needs to get some rest." He walked around the table to his sister and kissed her on the top of the head. "Don't drink too much and don't let this one get you into trouble."

Casey wasn't looking at Troy, but I was, and when he said that, Troy nodded and took a drink.

"I won't. I'm going to drink this and head back over. I need to start over on my project," she said solemnly.

"Good night, guys." I yawned as I turned toward the house.

"Thanks for dinner. Your ribs were killer," Troy added rubbing his belly, stretching out and propping his feet up on my empty chair.

"Night, Blake. Thanks," Audrey added.

Casey's and my evening ritual was becoming routine. I loved it. We'd brush our teeth. I tried not to be crazy creepy, but he sort of had a way of doing things. He'd take off his clothes and put on a pair of shorts to sleep in. He'd stretch his neck while he pulled back the blankets. After I climbed into my pajamas, I'd claim the remote. He always waited for me to get into bed before he climbed in. We went in together.

We were quiet, but when we'd catch the other looking, we'd smile at one another. The smiles were new too. Not *we're about to have reckless sex* smiles—although I think we both still enjoyed those. They weren't friendly smiles. These were smiles earned, fought for, and appreciated. We'd worked hard for these little moments and when our eyes met like that, for a split second we'd both acknowledge how far we'd come.

Unlike in my former life, where the old me and the other man in my life would find our sides of the bed and stay in them, Casey and I rolled into each other. My sheets were starting to smell like something new. Mixed chemistries. His and mine meshing on the fabric. He had a favorite pillow in my bed. My favorite pillow was the crook of his arm.

As we found our places, the spots where our bodies aligned, he sighed.

"So are you going to tell me what's up?"

It was now or never. Even though he knew the results of what happened, he didn't know exactly how. And with Grant playing even more games, Casey needed to be armed. I wouldn't let anything happen to the man holding me in his arms. He was full of good and love, and even when I'd damn near ruined us both by not accepting everything he wanted to give me, he never held that against me. He deserved my best. My very best. That included my honesty and trust.

"I talked to Reggie this morning," I began. My finger traced the words inked on his chest as I prepared myself for everything I was about to say. My foot linked around his leg and I was centered.

I drew another breath, and since he was waiting for me to continue, I let it all out.

"He said that there's a guy he knows at the station—I think he said his name was Paul. Anyway, this guy called him and said he'd heard that *he* may be changing his story. Apparently, it was suggested that pulling the gun was self-defense and maybe you were the one who hurt me."

He stiffened. Breathed. Then, held me tighter.

"The cop said that everyone pretty much knows that's bull-shit, but if it went down like that, there would definitely be a trial and Reggie thinks you'd be called in. Maybe arrested if *he* goes through with saying you did it all."

I kissed his shoulder and sorted through my thoughts. He moved me on top of him, and I folded my arms under my chin on his chest so I could look at his face. A storm brewed there, but he was doing a damn fine job of staying calm.

"I called Dr. Rex and told her everything. I told her what I remember."

His eyes looked a little relieved, but still turbulent weather swirled in them.

"I wanted her to have record of me telling what happened before it all got messed up. And I want to tell you too. I'm sorry that I've been saying I can't remember what happened. I was lying. Wasn't going to keep it to myself forever, just until I processed it. You know?"

He nodded and leaned up to kiss my arm. It was about the only part he would reach with me lounging on him like I was.

"I understand that. Believe it or not, I knew that's what you were doing."

"Plus, I knew it was going to hurt you and my family. It was awful, Casey. I wish I couldn't remember," I whispered, because my voice began to cut out.

I exhaled my hesitations and inhaled all the strength I could take in. His hands rubbed long, slow passes over my back to soothe me. His touch had magic in it and, in that moment, I needed his strength. I needed him.

"So you knew he told me he was signing the papers, and that's why I went that night. When I got there, he'd been drinking, and I should have just turned around. I was being stubborn. I just wanted it all over with. I'd been so looking forward to introducing you to my parents and my family that I was feeling a little high from it, I think. I thought if I could just get this done, it would be one less thing to worry about, and then we were going to celebrate.

"He'd put glasses out on the table like I was going to stay, but that was never my intention. He asked if I could at least have a drink with him, but I said I needed to go. When he started getting angry, I decided to leave, then he grabbed my arm and pulled me up the stairs. He said that's where the papers were, and that I wasn't leaving until I got my precious papers.

"I knew it was only going to get worse though. Something

told me that if I got to the top of the stairs something really bad was going to happen. He just kept yanking me."

I didn't have enough energy left to tell the story *and* keep my emotions at bay. My voice sounded shrill and high, and by that time, my face was hot with spilled tears. Casey never looked away. Caring and strong, he silently gave me support. I didn't want him to visualize it. To see any of it. Because the thought of him being in pain was unbearable to me. I could only imagine the hell that was seething inside him.

"He started pulling my hair and it hurt so badly, Casey. It felt like he ripped my scalp off. I just wanted to leave. I was scared you were going to leave thinking I'd fucked it all up again. So many things kept running through my head. I tried to hit him. I fought back, but it wasn't enough. Then he hit me in the face, and I thought I was going to pass out.

"So I did the only thing I could think of and bit him. I bit hard until I tasted blood. I think he swung at me again, but when I didn't let up, he let go and I fell backward. The expression on his face, when I was falling, wasn't even concerned. It wasn't anything. It was just blank. Like he didn't even care." As I fell I only thought of Casey.

I sniffled and Casey reached over to the nightstand to get me a tissue.

"Here you go," he said with such compassion. When I thought he was going to be enraged, and I'm positive he was on the inside, he was gentle and he cared for me.

I sat up and blew my nose. He didn't leave my side, sitting up with me.

"Are you okay?" he asked.

It had only been the second time I'd told the story and by no stretch of the imagination had it been any easier than the first. Watching Casey's anguished face, as I revealed step after step, had been agonizing. My heart was beating frantically, and my skin itched with each memory. I knew this was hurting him, and yet he asked me if I was okay. His quiet strength gave me the strength to answer him truthfully.

"Yes. I just want it to be over. I just want him to go away," I replied, finding some composure. Then I faced him. "But if he thinks he's going to hurt you, or cause you trouble, he has another thing coming. I won't allow it."

That was that.

Be a dick to me. Harass me. Beat me and knock me down. But it would be over my dead body before he did anything to Casey. That included trying to put blame on him where it most certainly did *not* belong.

"I don't want to go through a trial. I want to move on, but so help me God, I will. I'm thinking about going to the police and just telling them everything," I confessed.

He didn't say anything for a long time. He just sat next to me, probably wanting to kill him. The silence was too much to bear.

"What are you thinking?" I asked as we settled back down into the bed. I was exhausted from the day. From telling him what happened. From thinking about what I should do. So curling up into his side, I patiently waited for the soothing rumble of his voice.

"Just hold off on anything. I'll call the lawyer tomorrow and see what he thinks. The way he's trying to spin it is full of holes. Reggie was there with me. He was holding a gun and didn't put it down—even when the police told him to. Fuck. He was going to shoot me. Who knows what he would have done had he gotten you upstairs. Was he going to threaten you? Or worse?" He let out a huff of breath and the breeze blew my hair. "I can't even think about that."

"Well, what am I going to do? I can't let him push me around. I can't just accept him saying that."

"Shh, I'll take care of it. He's not going to do anything. Okay, honeybee? He can't do anything to us."

I wanted to believe him. I didn't know what Casey could do, other than go with me when I told my story, but I was confident he'd be by my side and I'd be by his. We'd figure out something. We always did.

We both lay there in silence. Thinking. Looking for an answer for a long time.

"Casey?" I finally said, drowsiness sweeping into me and swirling my thoughts to other things.

"Yeah," he said, holding on to me as I rolled over and put my back to his chest.

"I really want some chocolate cheesecake." Even as I heard the words come out of my mouth I knew they were random. Being tired sometimes does that to you.

"Then we'll get you some tomorrow. You just sleep."

Curled into his warm body, I fell off into a deep slumber. I'd told him what had happened, I trusted that together we'd be able to handle anything. Being in love might pack on twice as much trouble, but being in love with the right person—well, that's when you never have to carry anything alone.

We made an unstoppable pair. A team. A force to be reckoned with. I fell asleep feeling better knowing he was there and I was in his strong arms.

I'd dare anyone to test our love. They wouldn't stand a chance.

EIGHT

Casey

Tuesday, June 15, 2010

I DON'T THINK HE quite understood who the *fuck* he was messing with. I wasn't some chump who was going to let some bastard terrorize my girl. Terrorize me. Not when the biggest thing she should be worrying about was feeling better and trying to guess when I was going to put a ring on her pretty little finger. I wasn't proud that I'd stolen his girl, but I sure as fuck had. And I'd fucking ruin everything else in his pathetic humdrum life if he didn't back the fuck off.

Now.

No more was I wait-and-see Casey. The days of letting someone else determine any factor in how our future would go were over.

I called the shots.

I made the rules.

And it was time I *told* him how shit was going to go. Then enforce it.

With Blake soundly dreaming by my side, I lay in bed that night and plotted. I ran every possible scenario over and over in my mind constructing a plan. I wasn't able to protect her from him that night. That would never happen again.

Around one in the morning, I knew what I was going to do.

"Yeah, I'll tell her," I promised Reggie as we talked the next morning. I called him to see if he had any more information, while Blake was making coffee for Troy and me. He pretty much confirmed everything Blake said. I told him Blake confided in me, and I was surprised when he didn't ask for details—and I didn't offer them. It wasn't my story to tell. Besides, Reggie flying in to kill her ex-husband wouldn't do any of us good. And it would fuck up my plan.

"Good. So I'll see you guys this weekend. I'm coming in on Thursday to make my statement again, and I think Mom and Dad want to have an anniversary dinner since their party was postponed."

"Okay, I'll let you know how it goes. See you later."

It was pretty early, and I hadn't gotten the best sleep, but I was wired. My spine was full of steely determination. Even before coffee.

"You guys are going in so early." She yawned, still wearing the clothes she'd slept in.

"Early bird gets the beer," Troy joked as he zipped up his bag and set it by the door. "Hey, I still need to go pick up the car this morning. And not that your spare bed isn't comfortable, but I think I'm going to check into a hotel tonight."

"Good, you drank all my beer anyway," I jested.

I made my way around the counter to my girl and planted a quick kiss on her lips. Then I gave her another, because one small kiss wasn't enough. "I'll see you later. Call me if you need anything and wait on what we talked about last night, okay? I'll call you."

"Okay. I think I'll hang out most of the day, maybe see what Audrey is doing for lunch."

I'm pretty sure the little shit was headed back to bed. Or at the very least to lay on the couch and watch television. It wasn't quite six yet. I knew that's what I'd rather be doing. But I had shit to do.

I made one phone call on the way to the brewery. Troy didn't ask any questions.

"We're picking up your rental about ten," I told him. There was no doubt he could tell I was working things over in my mind, and by the sound of the message I'd left, today wasn't going to be a normal day at work.

I didn't ask much out of people. It was a rare day that I asked for favors, but I was calling one in. I needed Troy. Well, I needed someone and I had Troy.

Ten o'clock came and we'd picked up the car he'd arranged.

I sat in an empty booth waiting. I'd never done anything like what I was about to do. It's interesting about what they say *when push comes to shove*. I'd been pushed and pushed, but I had yet to push back. Learning what I had the night before was a shove. A deliberate, two-handed shove. That day I was doing the shoving. And someone would be flying right off the fucking cliff.

The bell rang above the door and since it was too late for the breakfast crowd and a little too early for people coming in for lunch, I assumed it was him. I looked at my watch. Apparently my message was loud and clear. My guest was on time to the minute.

I wasn't facing the door, but I didn't have to be. I heard his breathing. I listened to his steps. My blood boiled, but I put a lid on it. Every muscle in my body wanted to rage, to tear, to pound and maim. But my mind was focused with razor-sharp clarity.

This.

Motherfucker.

Was.

Mine.

Grant took a seat across from me and I sipped my coffee. I knew he'd show. He looked around for someone to serve him, but no one came out. That made me grin. It gave me pleasure watching him not get what he wanted, even if it was something as insignificant as a cup of coffee.

"Your message said you wanted to talk. Have you forgotten you have a restraining order?"

So it was going to start like that. He looked pretty normal, as I took stock of him and his goofy L.L. Bean wardrobe. He was lame. Even his clothes annoyed me, so I didn't answer. I was going to make him wait.

Taking another long sip from my hot mug, I stared at him. Ask me if I gave a fuck if it made him uncomfortable, which it obviously did by the way he ticked his finger against the Formica. I leaned back in the booth and tilted my head. I was being cocky. I was good at it.

"What the hell do you want?" he demanded after a few minutes, an ugly snarl on his face.

"I don't want anything from you. I have everything I've ever wanted. In fact, I'm here to offer *you* something."

This made him laugh.

Chuckle all you want, you piece of shit. We'll see who's laughing in a minute.

So I laughed with him. Mocking him was fun. It took my mind off ripping his throat out of his pompous neck and getting blood all over his predictable fucking polo shirt. The image was enough.

The bell above the door rang again and it snapped me out of

the homicidal thoughts I'd been fantasizing about.

After that day, I'd put it behind me. For the moment, I enjoyed it.

The newest patron sat behind me in the booth next to ours. I knew exactly who it was, but he didn't.

"What do you think you can give me that I'd even want?"

What didn't I have that he wanted? I'd start small.

"I'm offering you an easy way out. Sure, you've got a few other things you have to deal with. What was that? A resisting arrest charge? You'll be able to clean that up in a few months. I'm offering you a chance to get away with attempted murder, felony battery charges, and let's face it, probably a few more than that. So, in a way, I'm offering you your job, your family's reputation, your house, your friends—do you have any friends? Anyway, basically your life as you know it."

"I don't know what you're talking about." He played dumb.

I figured he would at first. I just needed to piss him off a little more.

"Maybe if you're lucky you'll find some other woman to show mild interest in and convince her to marry you. Hey, maybe you'll actually fall in love. Just like Blake and I did."

His eyes dilated. It wasn't about her; it was about his pride. His ego. His image. Losing. I wondered if he ever loved her the way she thought he did. Maybe he honestly didn't know the difference. That concept almost made me feel bad for the dick, but not quite.

"You have no control over that. In fact, I could offer you the same thing. I think the police may be contacting you about the home invasion I reacted to that night."

Liar, liar. Khakis on fire.

"You can say what you want. Do what you have to do." I finished my cup of coffee just as the sweet, older shop owner came back out. She walked over to the table behind me and took my best friend's order.

Troy had done exactly what I'd asked him to do. Be a pawn. Give an illusion. And for the moment, he was just some dude in the booth behind us.

"Exactly, we'll see what happens," he sneered.

I pushed my empty cup to the edge of the table top, and she topped it off as she walked by, not saying a word to Grant.

He might disagree, but I loved the service there. Paid the sweetheart to go along with my "practical joke" not to serve my friend. His face was priceless registering he'd been blatantly ignored. Fifty dollars well spent.

"See the thing is, your story only works if Blake doesn't remember."

"Well, she doesn't. That's what the detectives said. So now it's just your word against mine."

"And Reggie's. I doubt he'll soon forget the sight of his sister after what you did." I'd done a good job maintaining self-control, but thinking about that sight threw kerosene on my temper and topped it off with a match. "Don't you remember? The blood? Her passed-out cold, dead for all you knew? What was it that you said to her? '*Get up, you bitch.*' Yeah, I remember that, too."

I took deep breaths and did everything in my power to stay where I was. The urge to hurt him was powerful, but that wasn't the way. It was one of the ways. I'd considered them all. But it wasn't the best way for Blake.

"And?" he pressed, shifting uncomfortably in his seat.

"And she remembers all of it. The way you pulled her up the stairs, by her arm and her hair, when she told you she was leaving. The way you hit her back when she was trying to get away. She remembers how you snatched her head so hard you ripped the skin apart. You fucking bastard, she remembers it all."

His skin grew pale and he didn't move. His eye contact broke and now focused on the table. The second he knew he was fucked was validation. Was proof. Was insurance.

"So, you listen to me. You get off scot-free. As much as I'd love to see you rot for a few years behind bars—which still might happen if you don't weasel your way out of everything—she'd rather not ever look at your miserable goddamned face again. That's what she wants, but don't be mistaken—" I lifted the envelope, I'd had on the booth seat next to me, "—we will see you in court, if that's the way you want to go. It would be pretty incriminating to match her teeth to the nice bite on your leg, wouldn't it?"

I watched his eyes land on the manila envelope I'd brought with me. I leaned back and took another sip. He was playing right into my hand. There was dread and fear in his eyes.

"That, Grant, is her statement. Written by her and notarized with today's date. All you have to do is get the fuck out of my life and I'll let you keep yours. Because she's ready to do whatever it takes to make you go away. You can do it on your own, or we'll watch a bailiff escort you to your new address. Your choice."

After he thought about it for a little bit, I thought I saw him coming around to the logic of what I was offering him. But that dirty cocksucker still had a little fight left in him.

"It's still her word against mine and we both know she's not known for telling the truth." His voice held none of the power he tried to convey with his words. It sounded like an excuse. Like one last cheap shot. Cheap, just like him.

"Only she isn't lying and everyone knows it, and while you're in prison, we'll be having a wedding and a honeymoon and a life … and you know what the best part is? She'll only *ever* be thinking about me when I'm inside her."

"She deserved what she got. The cheating bitch is lucky that's all I did, but I should've shot you," he growled through gritted teeth. That would have made me lose my mind … if I didn't just get it all on tape. If I didn't know that I could ruin his life.

"Probably, but it wouldn't change anything for you. See, you've got this one chance. Just one. Understand me?" I stared deep into his icy, evil eyes. "Oh, and if you need any more persuasion," I added slowly, knowing that this would be it, "the guy behind me is Officer Paul Summers with SPD. He's been recording this whole conversation. Just in case I needed anything, you know, because of my restraining order."

Troy raised his hand, but didn't turn around. In it was a tape recorder and he pressed stop at that exact moment.

I hunched forward over the table and grabbed him by the ugly shirt in one swift movement. I spoke low enough for him to hear me with a tone that wasn't easily misunderstood.

"If you ever consider contacting Blake, her family, or me

ever again, I will beat you within an inch of your pathetic fucking life with my bare hands. No gun needed. Then I'll make what you have left a reality so ugly, you'll wished I killed you." I released my hold and patted his shirt flat. "*Capisce*?"

He didn't say anything, but I saw it in his eyes. I saw the surrender. That wasn't good enough.

I snatched him up with both hands the second time, even faster than I had before. My knuckles white as I lifted him out of the booth and onto his toes.

"I don't think you fucking heard me. Grant? Do. You. Understand. Me? Yes or fucking no?"

"Yes," he spat. "Yes, I understand."

I dropped him just like that, and walked toward the counter to look at their selections, while saying, "Good, have a nice life. You're welcome."

He didn't wait around and that was good for both of us. I exhaled to expel the extra energy that was wild in my veins as I heard the bell above the door chime. I hoped that was the last time I ever saw that prick, and something about the look in his eyes said he knew he'd lost and it was over.

My heart was pumping. I so wanted to hit the fucker, but I was fairly certain what I'd just done was the hit that would count. I felt good. Alive. As if I'd finally fought for my girl and won.

I looked in the glass case and saw exactly the one she'd want.

The lady came out and gave me I-know-that-wasn't-a-practical-joke eyes. I returned them with I'm-sorry-that-got-out-of-hand-but-my-honeybee-needed-help-and-you're-lucky-I-didn't-murder-him eyes. She swatted her hand towel at me over the top of the pristine glass case.

"I need two Quadruple Chocolates."

I looked over my shoulder at Troy, still sitting in the booth behind where Grant and I were sitting.

"Troy, do you want cheesecake?"

We both knew he'd just broken a law for me. A pretty big one too. Impersonation of an officer is serious business. I wouldn't have asked if it wasn't the only way. The way that could get him out of our lives. A way that Blake wouldn't have to worry about him anymore. Not ever again.

"Strawberry," he said, looking at me like he'd never met me before.

"Better make it two strawberries, four Quadruple Chocolates, and two of those pecan-y looking ones over there."

She packaged them up the way I asked her to and we were off. Troy with his cheesecakes in his rental, and me with mine. He was headed back to the brewery, but I still had one more errand. I hoped Blake's mom wouldn't mind if I kept honeybee's cheesecake in her refrigerator. I was bringing her some, too, after all. And if she were anything like her daughter, she'd do just about anything for it.

"So do you know what you're looking for?" asked the cheery-eyed sales lady. She'd been helping another woman when we first came in, but now her focus was set on us and the display case of engagement rings we were hovering over. I'd picked Blake's mom up to help me. My girl wanted to get married and far be it from me to make her wait any amount of time longer than necessary. Honestly, I wanted the same thing.

Her divorce was final.

Grant eradicated from our lives was final. I'd made sure of that. The look on his face said it, and when he voiced his consent, I heard it. It was even evident in the hunch of his angry, defeated shoulders as he left the bakery. I was through messing around with that shit-stain.

I think I might have even scared Troy a little. That or impressed him.

But all of that was over. What I wanted to remember about that day was that I found the perfect engagement ring for my honeybee. That her mom and I found one she'd cherish forever.

Kara Warren was a lady. She wore cream dress pants and a peach-colored blouse. She wore pearls and her hair was perfect and just so. I wondered if she normally looked so put together or if this was a special occasion.

Almost everything about how we'd met had been backwards. We were both wrecked when Blake had been in the hospital, but she looked really pretty on ring shopping day.

"We're looking for an engagement ring," she informed the clerk. Her smile was as bright as anything under the glass. "He's proposing to my daughter. I'm just here to help a little."

"My name is Samantha. It's my pleasure, right this way." The sales woman nodded like that was common and knowing what we were there to buy—men don't bring the mothers to browse—she honed in on us. She gave us her full attention, walking us to a small seating area. Kara and I sat on one side and she sat on the other of a mirrored desk. It wasn't the right time, but I thought about how nice it would be to get some mirrored furniture. Think of the views you'd be able to get while someone you loved bent over a table like that—naked.

"So what does she like? What's her style?" Samantha asked, trying to gather information. I looked to Kara and she pinched her lips to the side in thought.

"I think she'd like something simple and classic, but something unique too," I answered her, while watching Kara for confirmation.

"Yes, definitely something a little different. Blake has fun tastes in things," her mother coyly admitted, winking at me. She nudged my arm with her elbow indicating she'd been joking and I was the punchline.

"She must get that from you," I said to her as Samantha pulled up information on each of the stones she'd brought over to show us.

"Okay, I have a few things to show you, but also know we do have a gemologist on staff who can design anything you want. I'll take a few notes on what you like and don't like, and then see what we come up with." She excused herself and went straight to a case across the room, unlocking it with a key. When she returned she came with a fake black velvet hand and a black velvet tray hosting probably ten different styles.

"This one is called a princess cut ..." And that's probably about the time I zoned out. I mean, I half-assed paid attention when she spoke about quality and clarity and shit like that, but none of those rings were right. We didn't have an ordinary love, so she didn't deserve some ordinary ring. I wanted to see something and think, *that's it. That's without a doubt the one.*

That never happened.

I was a little disappointed. Had I expected to ask her that night? Maybe. Hell, I don't know. If it felt right. *Even* if it felt right, I knew I wouldn't if I didn't have a ring to seal the promise.

The trip wasn't a waste though. As we were waiting for Samantha to come back with her business card and the information about going the custom route, I saw a necklace in one of the cases we'd overlooked on the wall. A thin silver chain, so fine I could barely see the links, held a pendant and I immediately wanted it for her. A silver, or white gold—fuck, I had no idea—charm weighed down the center of it and a small diamond sat in the middle.

"Samantha, I'll take this, please," I called out, getting her attention as well as Kara's. We'd been there for two hours and I didn't have a single reaction to one ring she showed me, but this necklace was perfect.

"Casey, which one?" Kara whispered as she came to the case where I stood.

"The anchor."

"That's gorgeous; she'll love it. Have you bought her jewelry before?" Kara asked, linking her arm with mine.

"Nope. This is the first."

The first. There were firsts everywhere and it amazed me how after all this time, we had so many milestones left with each other. The first piece of jewelry I gave her didn't come with promises or obligation attached. It was just a gift, because it would look so pretty around her neck.

I'd taken her on a trip. She bought *me* ships once upon a time, and this twinkling pendant would be a good match for them. As Samantha took it out and held it in front of me to appraise before boxing it up, I realized how good buying things for her felt. It made me happy knowing I was giving *to* her.

Although the trip didn't result in a ring, I wasn't leaving empty-handed. And the necklace would go perfectly with what I wanted to ask her.

Things were lining up—well, a little differently than I'd planned—but it was clear where we needed to be. The anchor reinforced that for me and reminded me of one step I wasn't willing to hop over. One that would ensure we'd be together, from this day forward.

NINE

Blake

Thursday, June 17, 2010

FOR BETTER OR FOR worse, I had to wait.

I was trying to be patient. You'd think after waiting two years to be with someone, I'd have at least a thread of willpower. I wanted him to ask me. I needed him to ask me. It was the knowing without a doubt he was going to, but not knowing when, that was driving me crazy.

Each day I felt better and better, and it seemed as though I was healing from all angles. The reminders on my body were fading and I looked like myself. The small apartment made me stir-crazy and I wished we were in San Francisco. At Casey's house there would be lots I could do. I could work in the garden or plant flowers. Hell, even cooking was better there with the view from the kitchen. The kitchen in my apartment was fine, but it had no view. It didn't even have a window, unless you counted the top half of the storm door leading out back.

I was ready to move forward, full steam ahead.

Casey didn't say exactly what happened with the lawyer, but whatever it was, it worked. Nothing ever came of what Reggie's friend told him.

The lead detective did call again to speak with Casey, but he didn't have to go to the police station or anything. Casey asked if anything new had come from Grant's charges and remarkably, there was nothing to report more than he was pleading no contest to the resisting charge and he'd probably just pay a fine after some family strings were pulled.

That was fine by me. I didn't care what happened to him as long as I never had to see him again.

"Trust me, honeybee. He's gone for good," Casey had said. The conviction in his voice demanded I believe him. The look in his eyes left no room for doubt. Next to me, he was the second person who wanted to make sure Grant was out of our lives, and if he truly believed it was over—then it was.

Since my parents' party had been put on the back burner, we were all going to a nice dinner at the Fountain downtown to celebrate their anniversary. The restaurant was a fancy affair and I was just as excited about having a reason to be with my family and Casey—all at the same time—as I was about the food.

It felt nice getting dressed up. I'd bought a dress online earlier in the summer and, by the grace of God, it fit just right. It was a slate-gray halter dress with a collared neck. I knew Casey would love it because there was a lot of skin showing. I added a coral belt and heels, which I hadn't even realized matched perfectly until that afternoon. Some of my tan from earlier in the summer was fading since I'd mostly been inside, but I felt pretty. I left my hair down and fixed it in loose waves.

We'd showered together—a thing that was just becoming the norm—and thankfully I'd budgeted our time to allow for the extended shower … including the extra steam. As I looked in the mirror, I wondered if the extra glow in my cheeks was from the recent orgasm I'd had or if it was because I felt so good.

Dr. Rex had been right, though. Talking about the attack made it easier to put it behind me. She'd told me it was okay to start feeling better and that there was no time limit for feelings about this kind of thing. She said when women are emotionally attached to a person who's hurt them, it takes a long, long time to heal. Having felt so far past any kind of attachment to Grant, it was easier to move forward. Easier to deal with the emotions as they came. I was processing what needed to be analyzed and putting the rest behind me.

With a future to look toward, I'd gain nothing from letting the past stall it.

"You look smoking hot, Betty," Casey said from the hall as he passed the bathroom.

I was leaning over, applying gloss to my lips. I capped the tube and took my time appraising him. Warmth radiated from my chest to my throat as I looked at the expression on his face.

Love. Adoration. Sincerity.

He looked smoking hot, too. Only hot wasn't good enough. He looked edible. He'd gotten a trim that morning and his curls were tamed, lying perfectly as they should. He wore blue trousers, a pinstriped shirt with a white collar and cuffs, paired with a thin tie. What was it about a man dressed up that made you want to cancel your plans and strip him naked with your teeth?

"Look who's talking, Lou. You clean up nice," I replied walking out to meet him in the hall.

"Are you finished?" he asked, but didn't let me answer. "I think you're finished. You couldn't possibly get any better. Come with me." He walked us into my bedroom and stopped me in front of the bed. "Sit. I don't feel like waiting until we get back for this."

I sat as instructed and my stomach twisted.

Was it happening? Was he about to propose? Yes, Casey. Yes!

I ran my sweating palms over the comforter while he went to the dresser and pulled open one of his drawers. The one I'd cleared out for him only a few days before—and he was already using it to hide surprises? If I'd known that's all it would take, I wouldn't have waited so long to move my shit out of his way.

He spun around and hid something behind his back. His eyes were intensely green in that light and the smile on his face was one of my favorites. The toothy-not-holding-back smile.

"I bought you a gift, but first I want to talk to you about something."

I was going to vomit. I felt lightheaded. All of my senses blazed to life and I felt overwhelmed. Joy, elation and every feeling I associated with Casey was amplified.

Yes! Just get on with it.

He sat next to me on the bed and I swiveled around to face him. He put whatever it was behind him down and took my clammy-ass hands in his.

"Blake, I love you. I love waking up with you every morning. I love listening to you fall asleep. I especially love how you make me coffee before I leave for the day. I love helping you clean up after dinner, even if I feel like I'm going to gain a million pounds if I keep eating this good." He laughed.

I was about to scream yes before he even asked me. I tried to focus on the sweet things he was saying, but my concentration was all over the place.

His lips. His eyes.

My heart was even into it, pounding out yes in Morse code. *Y. E. S.*

"I don't ever want my stuff to be separate from your stuff. My stuff likes your stuff. Our toothbrushes are now having an affair. We can't split them up. I know this might sound crazy, since I'm so invested in this Seattle branch, but after these past few weeks, I really feel like this is the best move for us."

Yes. Say it. Ask me. I'm yours.

"Move to San Francisco. To my house. It'll be *our* house. We can keep this place if you want; we can even look for another house here if you want something close to your family and somewhere that's ours when we come back. I want my home to be yours. I want *that* to be our home base. We've been floating around for so long. I'm ready to slow down a little. But I've realized that house isn't my home without you in it.

"And if you don't like that plan, that's okay. We'll figure it out. But that's what I want. I know that's where we belong. That's where we drop our anchor."

It wasn't what I thought he was going to say and still, I was feverish with excitement. Just in a different way.

It made sense. Troy could stay here and look after Audrey. I was glad to go somewhere with little to no chance of running into *him.* I could work in either city, as could Casey now. We could live wherever we wanted. And when it came right down to it, I loved that house. I missed that house when I was gone. He was right. That was where we'd build our foundation.

It wasn't an engagement, but it was so damn close that I'd take it. I'd take it all.

Casey watched me closely trying to read my mind. His eyes bounced back and forth from my right eye to my left, like he was going to miss my answer appearing in one or the other. Anxiously waiting, he bit at his bottom lip.

"Yes," I agreed with an emphatic nod. "I really want to."

He shot off the bed like a rocket. He did some fist pumping, then quickly reined it in, sitting back down beside me.

I love making him happy.

"Okay then, now you get this." I saw the long box when he jumped up. He bought me jewelry. Not that I wore a lot, or that I'd ever really given a damn about gifts, but I couldn't help but be excited to see what it was he'd picked for me.

"Turn around," he commanded softly.

I heard the creak of the box as it opened and a few seconds later he was putting a necklace on me. He kept the pendant behind me so I couldn't see what it was, and then he walked us to my full-length mirror. I stared at our reflection. We looked good together. Like a couple. Like two people who had everything in front of them.

His long fingers spun the charm to the front and placed it on my skin.

An anchor.

"You see where this sits, honeybee? Right here," he said as he tapped my chest and my heart tapped back in response. "It didn't really matter if you said you'd move there or if you wanted to stay here. This is my home. This is where I want my anchor. Right in here."

I didn't turn around, but I looked up at him over my shoulder. He looked content and strong and so damn handsome.

"Kiss me, Casey," I requested and he did.

He kissed me slow and tingles spread through my veins like fireflies glowing in the summer grass.

So much for being on time to dinner.

We weren't *that* late, but the restaurant was buzzing with dinner traffic. When we walked in we told the hostess we were meeting a party already seated. She smiled at us, relieved, as she continued with the people in line, taking names and head counts. We walked through the bar and paused at the main entrance to the dining room, where I scanned the guests for my family.

"I see them. They're over there," Casey said in my ear.

He placed his hand on my arm to steer me that way.

My blood ran cold and I froze in my spot.

No. Not again.

My arm. The same arm Grant had .... *Let go. Please let me go. Please.*

"Don't." I pulled away almost automatically. His eyes met mine; he was confused. "Don't pull my arm." *Let me go. Don't touch ...*

Casey stopped immediately, letting go before the words were even all the way out. My feet didn't want to move. *Couldn't* move, like they'd been filled with lead. My head knew I was all right, but my body disagreed. My thoughts conflicted with my actions. Reality blurred with memory.

"Hey, I'm sorry. I didn't think. Did I hurt you?" he asked, his eyes flashing with concern as the realization of what just happened dawned on him.

I needed a minute. I saw my dad on the other side of the room, but he was the only one who'd noticed us.

"I need a minute, okay? I'm going to go to the bathroom." I forced my legs to go and marched as fast as I could to the ladies' room.

What just happened?

He wasn't hurting me. He wouldn't ever ... it wasn't his fault. His grip on my arm was only guiding, not forceful or dominant. *He'd been so gentle.* I washed my hands and took a few deep breaths. I just needed to get my racing heart to chill out and I'd be fine.

After a few minutes, I felt my insides settle back into their places. I came back to myself. Back to reality.

I was safe. I was happy. I was moving forward.

When I came out of the door, I noticed Casey sitting on a bench at the end of the hall. Head down. Hands locked, thumbs spinning around each other. When he saw me he stood, but he didn't walk to me. He waited and I came to him.

"I'm sorry, Casey," I apologized. The expression on his face was pure worry and guilt. I hated that I'd reacted like I did, but it was out of my control. "You didn't do anything wrong."

"Don't apologize. I should have known—" he started, but I shut him up with a kiss. I tried to tell him I was okay. That it was over and I was fine in that kiss. I tried to kiss away the discomfort the situation caused. We were there to celebrate, not to freak out over nothing.

"Stop. I'm fine. Let's go have dinner. They're waiting on us." I took the lead and linked our fingers together and pressed my lips to the top of his hand. "I've wasted enough time freaking out, now let's have some fun."

When we got to the table, everyone stood and I hugged my dad first.

"Everything all right?" he asked privately in my ear.

"Yeah, I just had to go to the bathroom." It wasn't a complete lie. I did have to go in there—to get my shit together.

After all the hand shaking and hugging, we sat down to a family meal. Everything fell back into place. Casey was a great fit with everyone. They talked with each other like they'd known one another for years. I watched as my mom and dad held hands above the table. It looked so different than it had a few years ago. When I was comparing what I wanted to what they had. Or what it looked like.

Things had changed. It wasn't about "being like that" anymore. It was about how I felt, not how it looked like I felt—and what I felt was unquestionably right. I think they saw the difference, too. No, not saw, felt. We felt the difference.

We ate dinner the Warren way. Appetizers and shared plates of entrees. I think Casey liked it. He sampled everything like the rest of us.

"We have some news," I announced toward the end of the meal and the table fell silent. They were probably expecting what I had. "I'm moving to San Francisco. Casey and I are going to live together in his house."

Casey ran his hand over my thigh under the table and the combination of that moment being real and his big hand against my skin thrilled me.

"Congratulations, you two. He showed us pictures of it a few weeks ago when you were sleeping. It looks beautiful," my mother noted with a big smile. "And I love your necklace." She winked at Casey. Those two had been shopping together.

You don't take your girlfriend's mother to shop for necklaces.

"Thank you, it was a gift," I explained, but my mother, the secret keeper already knew.

My brothers and I gave my parents the present we'd planned to give at the party, a trip to Vancouver. It was a wonderful night. We drank champagne and laughed.

"Would you like to see our dessert menu tonight?" the server asked as we were winding down. I wanted dessert, but I was stuffed. Plus, I wanted to get home and celebrate our milestone in private.

"Boys, do you want anything? We're fine," my mom said.

"No, I'm good," Shane answered, rubbing his stomach.

"No, thank you," added Reggie.

"Well, what about us?" I asked. What if we wanted some?

"I have your dessert right here," my mom told me as she picked up a little brown bag she'd kept hidden between her and my dad. "Casey got this for you, but forgot it at our house."

I looked back and forth between them. They *were* together. I hadn't imagined it.

Then, like she'd said something wrong, she clarified. "Your dad needed help with something earlier and Casey swung by."

Fibber.

"Thanks for bringing it," he crooned.

"Well, if that'll be all, you're all settled up. I'll be back with your receipt, Mr. Moore," the waitress explained as she walked off. He surprised us all with that one.

"Happy anniversary. I hope we're as happy together as you are." He tipped his chin admiringly to my parents as he got up. "Now, if you'll excuse us, I've got a long day tomorrow. I hope you don't mind if we head out?"

"Thank you, son," my dad replied, and nobody made a big deal of it, but my heart squeezed as my dad grinned at the man who made my world spin.

My love for him would only grow and mature and that wasn't a promise. It was a privilege.

TEN

Casey

Thursday, June 17, 2010

IT WAS A HUGE privilege to see the pride my girl had at dinner. Her head held as high as her spirits.

"So what's in the bag, *roomie*?" she asked from the passenger seat on the drive back to the apartment.

"Your dessert," I said as nonchalantly as I could. I loved that she hadn't opened the bag. However, she had to know. I could smell it through the paper sack since her mother handed it to her.

We'd had a great night, aside from the episode when we

first arrived at the restaurant. The look on her face when I'd touched her arm had turned my hot blood into ice in my veins. I never wanted her to look at me like that again. Ever.

Pure fear. Panic.

Since she'd told me about what *he* did to her, I should have known not to grab her, no matter what. I hadn't been rough with her, or even aggressive, but I knew now there were triggers that would probably pop up over time. Aside from talking to Dr. Rex about it, I would have to be even more careful with her.

I could do better. Even though she was on the mend and I had no intention of causing her discomfort, I had. Clearly, there was still a lot of healing left to do. And I'd help her do it one inch at a time. It would be my pleasure—my mission—to erase what I could of that night from her memory. I didn't want my touch to ever frighten her.

How could a woman who was so strong, be so fragile at the same time? I guess we all were.

Those were thoughts for another time because in the car she was smiling and enjoying the night. It was time for celebration. For firsts. For good things.

"I know what's in there. It's all mine," Blake teased. "This reminds me of something." Then she giggled, thinking about the first time we'd shared cheesecake.

"I kind of remember winning a piece away from you last time."

"Mr. Moore, I'd love a rematch. I feel like I'm better prepared this time."

"So you still like Quadruple Chocolate? I thought you might be on to something else by now." Animated and carefree, she knew what she was getting into. I loved our games.

"Lou, I know a good thing when I see it. I *absolutely* still love Quadruple Chocolate, and I'm prepared to defend both of my pieces this time." She got as close as her seatbelt would allow and whispered in my ear, "And I'm very hungry."

Oh, fuck. My cock loved that. Time proved that my girl's dirty talk was improving.

Focus on driving, Casey. Focus.

The last thing I wanted to do was cause an accident. I needed to get her home safely, inside of her bed. Nothing was more important than her safety, but a close second was getting my cock there safely, and then getting it inside of her.

Safety first.

It was apparent she had no care for my cock's safety whatsoever, because when her hand traced the bulge in my pants, I damn near killed us all.

"I love your enthusiasm, Blake, and I look forward to the challenge, but if you don't leave my dick alone, I'll be forced to pull this car over." I stopped at a red light and turned my head just enough to feel her breath on my lips. "And if I fuck you in this car, your precious cheesecake may not survive."

She laughed and put her head on my shoulder, thankfully letting me drive her—and my defenseless penis—home. However, the little shit continued to talk smack.

How had I managed to find a woman who was as ornery as me?

"All right, Mr. Moore, I see what you're doing. You're afraid of my A-game and you need time to get your defense in line." She patted my leg. "But when the front door shuts, you better be prepared. I want that chocolate and I want it *bad*."

I didn't drive recklessly, per se. But I was only using the speed limits as a guideline. I'd learned my way around her neighborhood. The drive back was short.

She looked like an angel, but I didn't miss the extra sway of her ass as she sauntered to the door, not waiting for me. One hand held the bag; the other held the key, which she'd had ready three blocks back.

Oh, my fucking God. She was perfect and she really loved that damn chocolate cheesecake. It was almost a shame to move her away from it. *Almost*.

I'm sure San Francisco had something to rival it. First thing on the list when we got settled in: find it. Every man needs to know his woman's weakness.

Quadruple Chocolate was hers. She was mine. You do the math.

The door was open by the time I made it around the car. She stood holding it for me in that sexy-as-fuck half-librarian, half-vixen dress, as I walked through the threshold. She shut it behind me and I heard the lock click.

I loosened my tie.

It was about to get real. Real hot. Real intense. And real fun.

Blake walked past me into the kitchen and promptly put the whole bag in the refrigerator.

"We don't want it to spoil. This might take a while," she said, her voice thick with need. Hell, I hoped some of that need belonged to me and not just the cheesecake. It didn't really matter. I'd fly that shit south every week for this kind of attention.

Her fingers went to work on the buttons on the front of her dress. My fingers itched to do it for her, but my eyes loved the show.

"You see, I've been craving something, Casey. In fact, just thinking about it is making my mouth water."

I kicked off my shoes and she fought off a smile, doing her best to stay in seductress mode. I stepped toward her. It was going to be a showdown at the Cheesecake-sex Corral.

"Blake, there are just too many things I could say right now. You talk a good game, but talk is cheap." When I got to the hall, I walked backward toward her room. Stripping as I went. Her eyes followed my hands as they mirrored hers, button for button. I slipped the shirt off, but chose to leave the tie. You know. Something new. Throw her off.

She pulled her dress over her head, careful not to strain the still tender muscles.

That's it, honeybee, take it all off. Let me see that fucking body.

I was familiar with her in the nude, but seeing her in the white lace bra and panties she wore about stopped my heart. She looked flawless. Her lips were still plum and shiny from the gloss she'd reapplied earlier. Her chestnut brown hair fell perfectly across her shoulders. I wished I had a camera.

Then she admitted, "I wish I had a picture of you wearing just those pants and that tie." I bit back the laugh rising in my throat from our almost identical thoughts. Those moments always caught me off guard. Sometimes it was like she read my mind. My dirty, filthy, heathen mind.

She stalked toward me. Oh, hell was I lucky.

I sat on the bed and waited for her. I wanted her to climb on top of me and earn that dessert, but she had other ideas. Tossing a pillow from the bed on the floor, she knelt in front of my parted legs. I leaned back on one elbow and ran a hand through her hair. I loved when she was playful like this.

As she worked at my pants, I said, "Thank you for moving in with me. You make me so fucking happy." It was odd in the moment; we had this whole sex battle brewing, but I meant it. I had to get it off my chest, and I really wanted her to know.

"You're welcome," she said concentrating on my briefs. I lifted for her to pull them down. I was about to get a blow job—probably a damn good one at that—but suddenly my heart was feeling something else. Then she looked up at me, big brown eyes, nose flushed my favorite pink and added, "But sweet talk and jewelry aren't going to get you a piece of that cake, Casey. Now tell me what you want me to do with your cock." Her hand slid up the skin of my shaft and back down.

I was at a loss. My heart was somewhere, clambering on about mushy love stuff in my chest, but you know what? I could barely hear that fucker anymore. It was drowned out by my dick saying, "Tell her to suck me! Tell her right now, you jackass!"

I coughed as I watched her tongue sneak out and dip low behind my manhood. She never broke eye contact as she licked up the length of me. The sight of her opening up and slipping me into her mouth was the best thing I'd ever seen in my life. That record was quickly shattered by the closely followed maneuver of her taking every inch of me down to the base—eyes still on me, mind you—and she shook her dirty head while she moaned.

My balls went into production mode and tightened. They

knew they'd be working third shift that night.

I still hadn't said anything. I couldn't speak. I couldn't blink. The dick-sucking spectacle had paralyzed me from my penis out to every limb. I'm not kidding. I could only feel my cock and her mouth. Up and down she went. Sliding over every ridge, swirling her tongue around me when she topped my head. Her hands finding purchase where her mouth left a wet absence. She was unmerciful.

My stomach quaked and tensed.

She lifted her head up and pulled mine down with the tie, bringing our mouths close. Then whispered, "If you don't want me to eat all that cake, you better fill me up. Don't make me wait. I'm hungry."

Then the minx went back down on me. Licking. Sucking. Running her teeth lightly over the command post for every nerve in my body. With her free hand she placed my palm behind her neck and then she took me all in. She pulled on the tie and I held on to her without applying any pressure. I let her run the show. Fuck, she was doing just fine.

She moaned as I twitched between her beautiful lips. My body tensing as I felt come inch its way up my dick and into her hot mouth.

"Ah-ah," I breathed. My legs flexed and I came up off the bed, Blake still sucking every ounce I had to give. "Oh, God. Jesus. God." It was the most religious cheesecake sex war experience of my life. Sure, it was only my second cheesecake sex war, but that would be hard to top. She was a fierce opponent.

Her grip loosened on the tie and she pulled away from me wiping her open, sinful lips with her thumb.

I'd need a moment before my empire was ready to strike back, and mark my words it was going to strike. Hard.

I helped her up and kissed her. There is much to be said about kissing a woman so shortly after she's ingested—to my estimation on feelings alone, nothing short of three gallons of come, going on pure pleasure alone—but I didn't give a fuck. She was the sexiest thing I'd ever witnessed. Eyes red and a little glassy, cheeks flushed the same pink as the center of her face. Lips swollen and wet.

I laid her down and all the play was gone from her expression. There was only lust and me in her eyes. The game was probably over, but there was no way in hell it was a forfeit. I'd play her body until the buzzer.

I kissed her stomach and noticed her bra was the clip-in-front kind. She knew I liked those. I swirled my tongue around her navel and freed her breasts without even looking. I filled my mouth with her left breast as I moved between her legs.

I painted her with kisses. Her neck. Her chest.

I propped myself above her with one hand and my other found her damp panties. I gave them a little tug and her mouth fell open. I filled it with mine, then slipped my fingers under the wet silk she had between her legs.

She was shaved, all but a little patch at the top. I really liked that, and my recovering dick unquestionably loved it.

As much as I wanted her, as much as I needed her, I had to be careful and take my time.

It was always marvelous watching her body respond to me. Seeing how it conceded to my touch. With only one finger touching her clit, ever so lightly, I stroked her like that until she was almost bucking.

Patience, honeybee.

Although, I was a terrible example of patience. I blew my load before the sheets were warm.

They were warm now.

I teased her with my hand over and over, bringing her just to the point of madness. Then I'd back off just enough to keep her at bay. She wasn't the only greedy one in our bed that night. I wanted to taste her and feel her come on my tongue just as she had me. I leaned away and pulled her delicate underwear off, and my lips found their way to her sex.

She was sweet and already so close. Her flesh plump and ripe for me. Selfishly, I wouldn't make her wait much longer because *I* was greedy for her pleasure.

It didn't take her long.

A long lick up her center. A flutter at her clit. Two fingers coaxing her orgasm from the inside out. Then she was there.

"Casey," she panted. "Casey. Yes. Yes." Followed by the most ego-stroking moans a man could dream of.

It was a beautiful thing, the female anatomy. Where I needed a few minutes to recuperate, she had the ability and luxury of blissfully going and going. My hand never left her until I was positioned at her opening. Even then, I slid my thumb over her pulsing clit as I slowly sunk inside.

I looked down at her, the sweat gathered at her hairline, how the rose color had spread outward from her nose to every surface of her skin. Pink everywhere. Her eyes were focused on mine, but in a dreamy way. The look was both at me and through me at the same time. Maybe she was looking deeper. Maybe she could see all the way inside.

I kissed her forehead and pushed a hand under the pillow beneath her head. Our bodies did the rest on their own.

The friction.

The grind.

The hold we had on each other.

Our breathing paired just like the rest of us. *In and out. In and out.*

Until we both came again. Her hands clutching my hair. My face buried in her neck. And long after we were finished, we still lay like that, joined like prize-winning Siamese cheesecake sex-war fighters.

"You get two pieces," I mumbled into her hair.

"No, I'll share one," she relented, still out of breath.

"Okay, you have to go get them though, because I'm dead." I rolled over and pulled out of her. "My legs don't work."

She laughed, a most satisfied sound.

My dick considered round three.

I most certainly noted the weeble in her wobble as she padded off toward the kitchen. She wasn't running at maximum capacity either.

Game well played, Casey.

Then I heard her shout, "You fucker, there are four in here!" And I laughed until it hurt.

I was learning, and even though there were going to be rough patches, through sorrow and joy, we'd always be like this. We'd *always* be Betty and Lou.

ELEVEN

Blake

Monday, June 29, 2010

SAN FRANCISCO WAS GOING to be home base and surprisingly, it made me feel much more at ease. Relaxed. It felt like home. Like where Betty and Lou belonged.

Together, over the summer and even before my divorce, we'd started replacing some of his mom's decorations with art and pictures we'd chosen. It hadn't felt odd that way. Doing a little here and a little there. I think even then we both knew we wanted to be in that house.

That afternoon, while Casey was on a bike ride, I decided to begin going through Deb's bedroom. Casey told me he'd always planned on going through his mom's room and packing things up he wanted to keep and bagging up items that could be donated, but never got around to it. I knew it wasn't an easy thing for him. How could it be?

He'd asked for help with it before, but for some reason that day it was calling to me. The room smelled different than the rest of the house. It was sweet and inviting, not that the home wasn't, but it smelled like a mom, the faint hint of what was probably her favorite perfume still lingering from the uncapped bottle on her dresser. It wasn't my kind of scent, but it was lovely and made me think of roses, which I knew she loved by the sheer population of them in her yard.

I bet being there, with all of her treasures and things that were totally her, made him miss his mother even more.

I brought in a few bags and a plastic tote to sort out what should stay and what could go. Ultimately, Casey and Cory would make sure I hadn't thrown out anything sentimental, but I had free rein to clear the room.

Her dresser drawers were orderly and everything had its place. Some things, I didn't even think twice about pitching, while other things, if I had any inkling it may be important, I'd put aside for their decision.

I opened up the closet, where many of her things were already packed and sorted, then lugged box after box to the basement. The few that were labeled *pictures of the boys* I opened and rummaged through.

She was a wonderful mom. It was obvious. I thumbed past years and birthdays, holidays and vacations. So many good memories she must have had.

It made me sad that I'd missed out on time with her. Knowing Casey's dad the way I did now, he definitely got his mischievousness from him. But I'd stand to bet he got his great big heart from her.

Finally I got to a little box on the top shelf.

It startled me actually. The box was yellow and embossed on the lid was a bumblebee. Chills ran down my arms. I blinked a few times to reassure myself I wasn't imagining it. Maybe honeybee wasn't just me. The box had to be a coincidence.

I set it aside, deciding to go through it last. There was something about it that was a little haunting and a little magical too. I turned up the music on my iPod. Sure, it was probably nothing, but a voice inside told me to wait. It gave my imagination something to think about as I put the last of her clothes in the bags and made sure each shoebox had a pair inside. I hauled things to the basement and took some to the garage for easy loading to take to Goodwill.

I'd been in there for hours, but the room was suddenly bare and wiped clean of someone having lived in it. There was a naked bed, the linens stripped and already hanging on the line to dry. The dresser empty of possessions and trinkets, most kept and set aside for future examination. All that was left was the box *and me*.

Someone so vibrant and dear lived in that room, and even though she wasn't my mom, I felt attached to her because of my love for Casey. In some respects, emptying her room was like losing her all over again. I could understand why Casey couldn't bear to do it.

My watch said it was almost five, so I decided to hold off on opening the box. The more I considered it, the more I thought Casey should open it. My instincts said it was personal, and I didn't want to infringe on something that was dear to her without permission.

After working on the room for most of the day, I carried the box and a bottle of water with me to the back yard in search of inspiration for what to whip up for dinner. Earlier, I'd noticed the tomatoes we'd replanted looking ripe, and as the strong smell of the basil entered my nose, it was almost decided for me. Margherita pizza was on the menu.

I abandoned the box and my water on the patio wall. As I took the flagstone steps down to the garden, it was as if my stomach was leading me.

The plants were thriving. Kind of like us, I guess. I'd taken a lot of pleasure tending to them and watching how well they grew. It was peaceful and gratifying to eat something you'd planted yourself. I understood why Deb had loved it so much.

Absentmindedly, with my earbuds in, I plucked a cucumber, and a few peppers that were ready, then snagged a stubborn weed that had managed to escape me that morning. I danced around, shaking my ass to Madonna until I got to the end of the garden where the tomatoes were, and picked two that would be just perfect.

This was my home.

When I turned around my breath was stolen.

On the patio, with his back toward me, Casey was on his knees, the small box beside him. My bare feet made short time from where I was to him, and I took the stone steps two at once.

I ripped the buds from my ears and tossed the vegetables on the table quickly to see what was wrong.

Then he looked up at me, through smiling tears he quickly wiped away. A hint of something shiny was in his hand.

"Did you read this?" he asked quietly, holding a piece a paper.

I crouched down beside him; my eyes searched his for what was happening.

"No," I said and then I saw the ring.

This was real.

He set the paper down, inched closer to me, and pressed a kiss to my lips, so fevered. So full of love it poured straight into my soul and doused any fear that had started to bloom from seeing him like that. His tongue swept across mine and he moaned, deepening the connection. Then, just as fast, he parted from me and pulled in a lungful of air and exhaled through his mouth.

"I think you're supposed to stand up for this," he said sweetly and gave me the most gorgeous smile.

Casey was an extremely good-looking man. Captivating even. But I don't think I'd ever seen that expression before. It seemed to be filled with adoration, vulnerability, peace, sincerity, and naked love. Stripped bare and honest, just for me.

In all my life, I'll never forget it.

My heart leapt first, bringing me to my feet. My body, as always, obeying his every command. As I stood above, my fingers found their way into the back of his hair and his arm wrapped around my legs.

Then he spoke. "Here goes nothing. Oh. I'm nervous." The levity of his humility and the joy in his laugh confirmed that this was it.

"I love you, Casey."

"I love you, honeybee. So much. And there were times I thought I'd love you alone for the rest of my life. Loving you forever would have happened whether I got to keep you or not.

"My love for you owns me. It consumes me. It makes me reckless and sane, with it I'm both weaker and stronger than I'd ever be without it. And you love me too. I see it in your eyes when you say it. The proof is in your touch. I was made to make you happy. To protect you. To keep you satisfied.

"I want you to be my wife, I want to be the father of your children. I want to remind you every day that we have something so special it feels blessed. It's torture and terrifying to love someone this much. And the miracle of you loving me back, I'll never take for granted.

"Will you please let me be yours—your best friend, your partner, your man, and your husband? Will you please make every fantasy I've ever had come true and marry me?"

"I've never wanted anything more in my whole life."

He stood and held the ring between his trembling fingers. Automatically, I gave him my left hand. He slid it over my ring finger and, like it was meant to be, it fit. I didn't even have time to study it. He wrapped me up in his arms.

In that very second, where I'd thought I'd given my heart to him before, I stood corrected. Because, as a trade for the ring on my hand, I unconditionally gave him my heart *and* soul.

Desire flooded every cell in my body. It had never felt that strong. That powerful. That tangible. I was in his arms and holding on to him with everything I had. How was it that even after he'd just given me everything I ever wanted, I wanted more?

Casey carried me through the door—vegetables forgotten, box forgotten—and pushed me up against the wall in the kitchen. He'd just claimed my heart and now I craved for him to claim my body.

His breath in my ear, he pawed at my flesh as his hips ground into me. My legs held tightly to him, wrapping around and locking at his strong back. I broke away to tear off my shirt.

He looked hungry. He looked ravenous. He looked like he was about to rip my skin from my bones to feast on my soul. And it was all his for the taking. Forever. Without any hesitation.

He moved us quickly to the island and lifted my ass to perch me there, needing his hands to wander where they pleased.

Pleased *him*.

Pleased *me*.

Pleased the universe and every god of love and lust and all the other gods who watched.

He cupped my breasts and rained kisses on my neck. Each one seared his invisible brand on my body.

"How, after all of this time, do I want you this bad? This much?" he panted.

It was as forceful as he'd been with me since … since before my divorce.

I'd missed his possessive touch. How much it excited me when he was carried away with desire and pleasure. The way his body teased my body to the point of begging. His natural dominance. The unapologetic way he made me buckle under his control. Always gentle with his power over me, and even more so lately. He'd backed off so far I'd forgotten how it felt to be his.

All the way.

Like this.

I wanted to give him everything. I wanted to be what he craved.

I'd said yes to being his, but I already belonged to him. It wasn't about conceding my will to his, it was knowing I had a will to give. That I was a whole woman. That I was *his* whole honeybee.

"Then have me," I breathed. "Have all of me."

He moaned, biting at my nipple through my bra. His eyes caught mine and I smiled. I wanted reassurance. That's the thing about dominance. If they're worthy of it, they don't take it. They wait for you to blissfully hand it over.

My hand raked through his hair and held tight.

"You don't have to treat me like glass."

His hands slid up my back and unclasped my bra. Then he tossed it to the side. Casey lifted me and pulled my yoga pants off in one fluid motion. Every move he made felt calculated and spontaneous at the same time, triggering sensations from every corner of my willing body.

"You have to tell me what you want. I don't want you to be uncomfortable," he said in my ear in the sexiest timbre. Then he moved my face to look at him and added, "Because I want to fuck the living shit out of you on this very counter. Then I want to take a shower and do it again and again, until either I die from an overdose of you or you say stop."

His words broke chains I'd tied around myself. Like only he could, he gave me what I needed. We traded trust. I trusted he would only love my body and he trusted I was ready for whatever he'd give me. And as my thirst for him grew, any residual pain I'd been hiding departed.

There's not much sexier than watching the love of your life lick two of his most capable fingers as he simultaneously unbuckled his belt with his free hand. Especially if the love of your life was Casey Moore. And lucky for me … he was.

I pulled his shirt over his head and he shook a long errant curl from his face. Inspiration hit me and I pulled the elastic from my hair and gathered the locks that seemed to be in his way. I gave him a ponytail as his two wet fingers found my center. He smiled once he learned the lick he'd given them was unnecessary.

I was wet. *As usual.* I was aching. *More than ever.* I was ready in every possible way.

Consume me.

With one arm he pulled me closer to the edge of the counter and I watched the muscle on his other arm flex as he grabbed his erection. Unlike the many other times where he'd stroke himself at my opening, he dove right in, and the sensation sent a spike of excitement to my core.

"Yes," I whispered.

He rushed my mouth and I invited him in. A kiss that could rival any kiss in history. His jaw working a rhythm that matched his hips. My head tipped back when my focus left and became incandescent with the rest of me.

His tongue slid down my throat as I lay back against the cold counter.

"Mmm," he moaned, "it's going to be a pleasure making

you come for the rest of my life, honeybee."

My chest rose and fell in quick succession as his pace quickened, the motion causing my breasts to sway. Like so many times before, I became wanton. Possessed. Only needing the releases that were imminent, both his and mine. Pure bliss streamed from my body to his and back like a current along a high-voltage line.

I watched him as he hypnotically gazed at where we joined. His eyes fell shut and his teeth sunk into his lip.

"Ahh," spilled from my lips.

Blue-green eyes snapped open and locked on mine, familiar with my sounds. One strong hand held onto my hip baring white knuckles, and his other hand swiftly came up to my clit. I watched, prepared for the sensuous touch he'd practiced so many times. But instead I felt a gentle tap and then another.

Then I was blinded with ecstasy as my orgasm unexpectedly skipped from slowly building to screaming in my ears.

I still needed more.

"Casey," I cried. "Fuck me. Harder, Casey." My hands gripped the edge of the counter and pushed back against him.

He leaned over and climbed atop the island with me, swinging my legs over his shoulders before he grabbed the edge of the granite behind my head and set a punishing tempo. It almost made me lose my mind. I clenched around him and rode a climax that felt like it may never let up.

"Fuck. Fuck. Fuck," he chanted until he yelled, "I'm coming! So hard. Ahh." He emptied himself inside me, his eyes screwed shut, and I watched as sweat ran down his beautiful face and fell on my lip.

He opened his eyes and like nothing had happened, as if we hadn't just left the stratosphere, mischief and happiness bloomed across his face.

When the second drop of sweat landed on my raw lips, I licked it and said, "Mmm."

I felt him twitch one last time inside me, and it made me giggle. I loved him so completely, without reservation. That would never change.

TWELVE

Casey

Tuesday, June 29, 2010

I LOVED TO WATCH her. How she moved. I adored Blake. That would never change.

I tried to memorize her every move, her beautiful ass swaying in the moonlight as she walked to the kitchen for water. The siren wore nothing but my engagement ring. It was the sexiest thing I'd ever seen.

The ring.

It was still messing with my head. How had my mother done that? How could she have possibly known? It was fucking trippy.

When I came home and saw Blake bopping around out back, I was drawn to her. When I saw the box on the stonewall cap, curiosity got the best of me. It was more than that though; my neck was in a collar and curiosity held the leash.

It was yellow. There was a bee on it. What the fuck?

First I'd thought Blake bought it or it was hers, and allowing the wonder to take over, I wanted to see what was in it. It was larger than a ring box, so I wasn't expecting what I found. When I lifted the lid, I noticed an envelope. After running my hands over it, I felt the ring inside.

To Casey, for your honeybee in my mother's perfect penmanship, brought me to my knees. I opened the envelope and examined the ring. A gorgeous, yellow diamond maybe? There were small, perfectly clear diamonds framing it, and the silver band shone like it had been bought that very day. The same day I'd been everywhere looking for the perfect ring—not taking a bike ride. After searching and not finding the right one, for so long, having it presented to me like that, from her, well it mystified me. There was something so right, so predestined about it.

Along with the ring inside the parchment envelope was a letter. I'd only read just a line or two when Blake discovered me standing there. There was no time to finish. I didn't want to wait another second to ask her.

I'd rehearsed the right thing to say. Fuck, I'd googled proposals. The time I spent looking for the ring added so much pressure for it to be just perfect. Not pressure from her, but from myself.

As I lay there in bed, waiting on my fiancée, I smiled knowing it was better than I could have ever planned. The look on her face was a mixture of elation and relief. Now I know why those YouTube assholes hire a video guy. Because when you really love a woman, you want to be able to watch that shit over and over. I'd never get to relive that moment, but I had the feeling there would be plenty more just as precious in our future.

And I'd watch her face light up knowing we were always on a course bound for forever together.

"What took you so long?" I asked when she climbed back into bed and turned on the nightstand lamp.

"Sorry, I was damn thirsty."

"Screaming like a banshee will do that," I teased.

"I'm glad your neighbors aren't that close," she admitted as a blush stained her cheeks.

I'd made good on my promise earlier. And then some. It turns out, proposals really turn me on. Or maybe her wearing *my* ring was the reason for the raging boner that wouldn't go down. Don't they say on those commercials to call a doctor after four hours? To hell with it. I hadn't seen a doctor to get that hard, so I wasn't calling one to make it go away. My dick knew what it was doing and that bastard was celebrating. *All night.*

Then I saw what else she had. The letter.

"Casey, the envelope says to you for me?" Leaning against the headboard, with no covers hiding her boobs, mind you, she stared at it mesmerized like I had. I stared at her boobs. She asked, "Casey, did you call all your girlfriends 'honeybee'?" Her jaw hung open like she'd seen behind the curtain at Oz.

I threw an arm around her and pulled her farther down into the bed with me. She didn't protest, only gazed into my eyes.

In the time I hadn't answered her silly question, her mind had played a trick on her.

"No." I kissed that cute nose and locked my leg with one of hers. "You're my first, only, and last honeybee. Now kiss on me a little."

The redundant answer pleased her; her kiss pleased me. We were two pleased-as-pie fools tangled in all-nighter sheets. Half ripped off the mattress, half wadded on the floor.

Blake looked like a queen when she beamed at me the way she was. Well, a queen with mascara under her eyes and completely fucked-up hair. I'm sure I looked just as good.

"Can I read it?" she asked sweetly, as she looked at the ring. "This was in there?" Her hand rocked side to side as the gem made a pretty reflection dance on the ceiling. We both watched the prism move, enchanted and love-drunk.

"You can read it, but are you sure you want to read it right now?" I asked as I rocked into her leg. Remember, it wasn't me. It was my cock. And he was ready to go again. I was really starting to respect his work ethic.

She wasn't helping the situation though. Her mouth found my ear and she sucked at it.

"Please?" she purred.

I would cave. She had the power to will me into whatever she wanted. All she had to say was 'please.'

"Okay, read it to me," I acquiesced.

"Thank you."

We sat up and I positioned her between my legs so I could peer over her shoulder. I propped my head in the crook of her neck and waited for her to start.

"Son, I've been fortunate to be your mom. You have the most beautifully wild heart. Charm for days and this magnetic quality that makes everyone immediately love you. I'm so proud. It's been my pleasure to watch you thrive and succeed. You and your brother have made me a very lucky mother. It's been the biggest gift of my life watching you turn into the men you are. I was blessed to see Cory find his love and, whether you know it yet or not, I know you've found yours, too. It's not my intention, or my style, to pry when it's not my business. But I've met her. Your Blake. Once at Micah's baby shower and again when Foster was born. The glow that poured out of her when she said she knew you, Casey, it was love. You'd be like a lock and key the way you two would fit together. Her energy felt the same as how it feels to be with you. It might not be the right time, and maybe you'll have to wait, but son, she's the one.

I've seen how you look through the photos of her on your phone in the waiting room when you take me to my appointments. I've seen the far-off look in your eyes when you're tired and thinking of her. I watched you scroll through her old messages once when you were sitting on the floor by me when I was a lump on the couch.

You call her honeybee, right? It suits her.

Writing this makes me so sad. I've tried to find the right words to make you go to her, but your heart is broken. Knowing the pain you're in hurts worse than the cancer that's eating me alive. I hope she heals you, for both of us.

I know I won't be there when you realize she's it for you, but I saw this in a wedding magazine that Micah left here. I called a jeweler and purchased it.

I might be way off and you might not be the one who finds this. But the thought that it's possible is helping me through the thoughts of not seeing it happen for you myself. Not seeing you grow into an even stronger man with love in your life, watching you become a father, and watching you love your family like I've loved mine.

I pray so damn hard that all of those things happen. It brings me peace believing they will.

So when they do, love her with all of your might. Love her until you feel like a fool. And let her love you back.

I won't be there to see what you do with this ring, but in some small way, if you find it and give it to her, know that it's the thing I most wanted for you ... and your sweet honeybee.

Love, Mom."

When Blake finished reading, through sniffles and emotion catching in her throat, she folded the paper and placed it on the table beside the bed and turned off the light. She turned in my arms and laid her head on my chest. Every few minutes she'd kiss my skin and I'd feel a tear roll across my skin and down my side. I stroked her back lazily with the ends of my fingertips until I felt goosebumps blanket her flesh.

And I thought.

I thought about how my mom hadn't told me how sick she was because she wanted to see me happy—specifically, with Blake. I thought about how I took care of my mother in those last days, and all of those times she asked me if I'd heard from Blake. I thought about how it was my mom's passing that brought Blake to me last October, and how those days seemed so far back in history I couldn't even feel how brutal the pain was anymore.

Moms are always right.

I loved my mom, what kid doesn't? I wished I had the chance to thank her. For her love, for her forethought, for always wanting my happiness, and for her generous heart. But for the first time since she'd left, I felt like I did something that would have made her genuinely happy.

Most of all, I hoped wherever she was, she knew.

I thought Blake would be reserved with the news of our engagement, as it's in her nature to be nervous of what others think. In that respect we were totally different. Where I'd slept that night with thoughts of calling everyone I knew—hell, I considered renting a billboard and taking out radio ads with the news—I just guessed she'd tell people, but in a moderate way.

Boy, was I wrong.

My girl beat me to the punch. While I was sleeping and dreaming of spreading the news, she was up doing it.

"I know and, Mom, the ring. I'll send you a picture. It's stunning. Absolutely perfect," she gushed over the phone. "I'm so happy."

Every single inch of me absorbed the sight and sound of her bliss. She wore my favorite tank top; the one I'd given her a long time ago. We both knew it was a one-sided gift. I could see her breasts through the long armholes when she spun around and caught me watching from the doorway.

"Yeah, he's up now," she said, laughing. "Sure, just a second."

Pulling the phone away from her ear, she wiggled her eyebrows and said, "She wants to talk to you. And good morning." She leaned over the island we'd scandalized the day before and kissed me as she handed me the phone.

Maybe I was still dreaming.

"Hello," I answered, clearing the morning gravel out of my throat.

"Good morning, Casey. Congratulations and thank you," she said as she choked up a little. "You're making my daughter so happy."

It was so sweet. I stuck my bottom lip out to convey what I could about what she was saying to Blake. She made the same endearing, pouty face back.

"Well, she's making me very happy too."

"Good, now let us know when you guys are coming back to town. I'm not sure what your plans are, and you don't have to have any yet." She chuckled and gave a little whoop. "Enjoy it and we're here for whatever you two need."

"Thank you, Mrs. Warren. We'll keep you posted."

"Call me Kara—or heck—just call me Mom." Then she went into a fit of giggles.

I laughed because she was laughing, and even though Blake didn't know what was happening, she fucking laughed too.

We called my dad, and called Foster and told him on speakerphone while Micah and Cory listened. Everyone was just as excited as we were. When people you love react like that it's hard to imagine you're *not* doing the most right thing on the planet.

The only one who cried at the news was my baby sister, Morgan.

"I'm sorry, it's just so … so … well, it took long enough," she'd said through audible tears.

News like that doesn't dull the more you talk about it. Not for us anyway. With every call, Blake bounced up and down. Every time someone squealed or shouted at the surprise, we joined them in earnest.

We sat on the patio that night after Blake made some pizza thing that tasted like it was delivered straight from Italy, and we drank a really nice bottle of wine my mom had in the small wine stash in her basement.

"To your mom," Blake toasted.

"To my mom," I agreed, lifting my glass and clinking it against hers.

Our families were really becoming one.

THIRTEEN

Blake

Friday, August 6, 2010

WE WERE BLESSED TO have so much help from our families, but I insisted I wanted to do it all. It was like I'd never planned a wedding. There were so many things I either ignored or didn't give two shits about the first time around.

Cake flavors. Bridesmaids *and* their dresses. Gifts for others. Places for the wedding and reception. The food. The music. The pre-wedding celebrations. There was a lot to manage. And I was enjoying every second.

Even though there was so much to think about, it was going smoothly and really fast. We'd be wed by the end of the summer and it couldn't get there fast enough.

"Which of these do you like?" I asked Micah at the dress store. My parents had flown down to San Francisco for the weekend and Mom and Micah were helping me shop. Something, by nature, I hated to do. But as the picture of our wedding grew more vivid with every decision, every detail, the more I got into it.

"I like the shorter one. So you guys decided on that place in Oregon?" she asked as she browsed through the rack of plastic-covered dresses.

"We did. Casey stopped in there last week on his way back from Washington and he loved it so much he paid the deposit on the spot, so our date would be saved," I said, laughing at the memory.

Blake, this place is fucking cool. You're going to love it. And I think I've got them talked into buying my beer. Well, the fucker is buying it wholesale and reselling it back to me, but what-the-fuck-ever. It's awesome. The pictures online are nothing compared to it in reality. This is the place.

That was all I needed to hear. In fact, it was shocking how much Casey wanted a say in all things of the Warren-Moore wedding.

"You guys are still cool with going there that week, right?"

Micah was my maid of honor. Again. She was the one wedding detail I was repeating. I loved her and she never once brought it up.

"Hell yeah, and we looked at stuff to do near the resort.

There are a bunch of activities we're going to take Foster to. It's going to be great. That place really is cool. Oh. My. God. We're going to be sisters!" she screamed when it hit her again for the hundredth time.

She was right. It was going to be great.

A creek ran straight through the property, allowing for hiking and biking. Casey loved it for the view. On the side opposite the creek, the Pacific Ocean in all its glory could be seen. Online we saw they had party tents to use and everything was so laid-back and beautiful. It felt surreal.

"Just six weeks, Blake. We have a lot to do," my mom reminded me as she rounded the corner holding a dress. "Do you want to try this on?"

"Mom, it's white."

"So what? It's beautiful."

That it was, but I knew that wasn't what I was looking for.

"I want the color creamier, less wedding gownish."

I expected her to protest, but she didn't.

"Less wedding gownish. Okay. Like flowy? Silky?"

"Yeah," Micah chimed in. "Something like this." The hangers screeched as she shoved the other dresses to the side and I saw it. It was much closer to what I was looking for. It wasn't exactly ivory, but instead a light buttery ever-so-pale yellow. It was form-fitting with a little mermaid flare at the bottom.

"I love it, but what I love and what looks right on me, might be two different things," I said insecurely. I went from not having a dress yet to praying the one we'd found, within only ten minutes of searching, would work.

I'd been having a good healthy streak of luck. There was no

way it would be that easy.

"Try it on, sweetheart. Let's see," my mom said calmly. "There's only one way to find out if it's the one."

I hated dressing rooms. They were always too small. The mirrors lied. There were never enough places to put all the shit you suddenly realized you were packing around like a mule. Regardless, my mom was right, I had to try it on.

I undressed and carefully folded my clothes, again totally not-typical behavior. I was nervous and stalling. I wanted it to look good. Better than good. After taking the plastic off and feeling the fabric, I really fell in love. It was smooth and flirty with a sweeping, open backline to match the deep cut in the front.

Slipping my bra off, I said a prayer to the wedding gods who I'd never spoken to before.

Please let this son of a bitch fit. Please let it fit. Please. Please. Please.

After a quick internal pep talk, I slid it over my head and it fell down my body. No resistance. No snags. No hang-ups.

I turned around to face the mirror again and there I stood: Casey's bride. My hand cupped my mouth and immediately I began to cry.

I felt beautiful. I felt overwhelmed. I simply stood there—vanity damned—and pictured his expression when he saw me in that dress. It wasn't until I heard Micah at the door that I snapped out it.

"What's it look like? Did it fit? Show us, dammit."

I pushed the door handle down and opened it, knowing she'd see my tears, but I was defenseless to make them stop.

"Oh, shit. Wow," she said on an exhale, as she backed up giving me room to come out. I heard my mother talking to a sales lady and I walked to her voice. Something inside me wanted her to tell me it was perfect. I needed her acceptance.

She dropped the shoes she was holding and her hands clasped together in front of her heart. The look on her face was even more than I wanted. More than I needed. It was all the confirmation I could have ever dreamed of.

"Oh, Blake," she mouthed silently. She walked slowly to me, her eyes glassy and her head tilted to the side. "Spin around."

I did as she requested and my hands flew out to both sides as I turned one and a half times, stopping for her to get a good look at the back, before I faced her.

"That's the first time you've *ever* looked like a bride." It was like she knew those were the exact words I needed to hear. I looked at Micah and she was smiling so big her dimples could have held water.

After we examined it in every light, and I wore it with shoes, we bought it on the spot.

Sometimes you find the perfect thing unexpectedly right off the rack. And if life had taught me anything, it was that just because it came out of nowhere, with no effort, didn't mean it wasn't meant to be. Kind of like how I found Casey.

With dress shopping done so quickly, my mom and Micah decided we should do even *more* shopping since our retail mojo was working in our favor. I went with it.

We took a break for iced coffees and I checked my phone.

Casey: Your dad is a fucking hustler.

Casey: Why didn't you warn me? I thought we were a team. He wiped my ass with the first nine holes and just made me look bad for fun on the second.

Casey: I hope you're having fun. I think we're all meeting at Cory and Micah's for dinner. I'll let you apologize for the humiliation and shame I've been subjected to later. I think I'll take a blow job. The start-to-finish kind.

I giggled and wondered if all couples talked to each other like that. Then decided I didn't want to know. I liked thinking it was only us. I quickly sent him a message back.

Me: Hahaha. Sucker. Warren domination. I didn't know we could use oral as a form of repentance. In that case, you owe me start-to-finish for listening to your dad talk about the 49ers for an hour straight the other night at dinner. I almost died from boredom. It was touch-and-go for about 59 minutes.

"Micah, are we having dinner at your place?" I asked. You know how guys make plans. It was very possible it was three-thirty in the afternoon and she didn't know she was hosting guests.

"Oh yeah, I forgot," she said as she typed on her phone.

She forgot?

"Well, it's getting late, so do we need to go get Foster or anything else?" I was clearly freaking out on her behalf. Her lack of interest was weird. She didn't even look at me.

My mom excused herself to find a ladies' room and I tried to get my friend's attention.

"Yo, Micah. It's like almost four," I urged.

"It's fine, Carmen has Foster. She's bringing him back this evening. I'm not stressing about it. I'll just order something in." She smiled brightly. "Quit worrying about it."

Me: Are you sure about dinner? I don't think Micah planned for all of us.

Casey: Yeah, I talked to Cory. He's grilling or something. We're heading there after a beer in the clubhouse. Get this. Your con-artist father is making me buy. Are you sure he's a professor and not in the mafia or secret service or something?

Me: Watch your back. I'll see you in a while.

Since I was the only one wigging out, I dropped it. Why bother stressing out if no one else was? It was just dinner after all. It wasn't like my parents were meeting his. We'd planned to do that the next night anyway. I was probably nervous about *that* and it was throwing me off. Would I ever stop feeling like the other shoe was about to drop?

"Well, thanks for having all of us over. Are you sure I can't do something?" I asked with less anxiety in my voice.

"Seriously, it's just dinner. It's no big thing. Now let's talk wedding night lingerie. What are you going to get?"

I hadn't thought of that. I'd have to add it to my to-do list.

I'm sure Casey would love to help with that one.

When my mother came back, we sat there for a while longer and talked about things that were seriously weird to discuss with a parent. But throwing me a bone, my mom kept her side of the conversation focused on silly fantasies with actors and musicians and left my con-artist dad out of it. I almost blew a good portion of my frozen caramel latte out of my left nostril when she admitted Casey was on her top five hottest men list.

I couldn't fault her. She had good taste. Maybe it was genetic.

FOURTEEN

Casey

Friday, August 6, 2010

GENETICS ARE FUNNY. BLAKE was a lot like her dad.

Even if he was a bastard who schooled me on the golf course, we shared the same sense of humor. Actually, we had a lot in common and he wasn't really a bastard. He was kind of awesome.

Phil told me embarrassing stories about Blake and he'd even had the foresight to save some of the most priceless childhood pictures of my honeybee on his phone for our day on the links.

He liked good bourbon, just like I did, and when we sat down after playing eighteen catastrophic holes, he informed me I was buying. He didn't hesitate to order from the top shelf for both of us. What a guy.

"All shit aside, Casey," he admitted, "I'm really happy for you guys. I've never seen Blake this happy and that's all a dad really wants for his kids. Above everything else in this world, you want them as happy as possible. You'll see."

Would I ever. The closer the wedding got the more I thought about kids. Every night we'd go to bed, and sometimes when we woke up, I'd bite my ready-to-reproduce-tongue to keep from asking her when she'd want to start a family. I didn't want to overwhelm her, with all of the wedding commotion going on around us.

We'd often joked about it, but I was serious. I couldn't pinpoint the reason why my desire to have kids with her was so strong, but it was. I really wanted a big family, like we both kind of had, of our very own. I wanted the hustle and bustle little hands and feet created in a house. I wanted my kids to grow up with Foster—and our families' future kids—for the plain and simple reason of it sounded like so much fun.

Besides, I enjoyed every moment we spent with Foster.

Now that dude was a cool customer. We had all of the same hobbies: Boobs. Getting dirty. Annoying my brother. A good sip here and there. I caught him taking a nap on my woman the other day, and if he weren't my nephew and godson, I would have been forced to lay the hammer down. He so easily stole the spotlight when I loved having it all to myself in her eyes.

Of course, all was forgotten when he said, "Ce-ce hug," before he left. He was smooth for almost two and knew damn-well how to work a room.

He got that from me.

So when Blake's dad brought up kids, the thought surfaced because it had been in the forefront of my mind anyway.

"Well, Phil, even though you could learn a thing or two about golf, you're a pretty damn cool dad. And I have a cool dad, so I know one when I see one," I joked, but I really meant it.

"I'll be honored to give Blake's hand over to you," he said between sips of his drink. "Are you ready for this?"

It wasn't my place, and I knew Blake hadn't talked about it with him yet, but maybe it would be easier for me to tell him what her plans were, with regard to aisle-walking.

"Oh, I'm ready. *So* damn ready. I've been chasing that girl for so long, and not that I wouldn't do it all again, but I'm definitely ready to start our life together." I second-guessed myself for a minute, then decided to wing it. I could read people, he'd be understanding.

Plus, if I broke this to her dad for her, she'd really owe me a start-to-finish thank you. I knew she'd been dreading it.

"Phil, can I talk to you about something that's been on Blake's mind? I know she wanted to talk to you about this herself, but since we're already here, you've already handed me my ass on my home turf and drank half of your grandchildren's college fund. I figure why not?"

He leaned forward and nodded.

I finished *my* half of his grandchildren's college fund and went to bat for my girl and what I knew she wanted.

"See, she loves you and she doesn't want to hurt your feelings or anything, but we've been talking about things that we want for the wedding. Specifically, and not that she'd come out and say it this way, but she doesn't want anything to be like the day …" I stalled.

I wanted to say the day violins almost ruined my hearing and my sanity. The day I thought I'd lost the love of my life forever. The day you handed her over to a piece of shit. But I settled for, "Well, you know what day."

After everything, after all was said and done, that wasn't her first wedding day, not in her heart and I wasn't going to call it that. I was just as stubborn as she was.

I continued explaining, when his eyebrow quirked up, challenging me to keep going. "Damn it, back then she felt so obligated. Not forced or anything, but like marrying him was what she was *supposed* to do. Everything was so messed up. We didn't know what the hell we were doing.

"I think she wants to know, and wants *me* to know, after everything we've been through, she's coming into this marriage on her own two feet. Does that make sense?" I ran a hand through my hair. It didn't feel like it came out right.

When I looked back up at the man who'd soon be my father-in-law, expecting him to be offended and probably a little hurt, that wasn't what I saw at all. I saw empathy. I saw compassion. I saw a father who gave a shit. I saw the kind of dad I wanted to be in the future.

"Son, didn't you hear me before? It doesn't matter if my little girl wants to have the wedding on Mars, the reception on Venus, move to Spain and buy an alpaca farm. If she's happy, I'm happy. Your wedding is no more about *me* and *my* feelings than ours was about my in-laws and what they wanted." He chuckled then added, "My father-in-law—God rest his soul—was a good man, but everything was his way or no way. End of discussion. So we did it his way. Our wedding was, next to the birth of our three children, the best day of my life. But if I had it all to do again, I think I'd have rather eloped."

In my eyes, her dad went from cool to Indiana-Jones-cool. I hoped when I was his age, in his position, I'd be as wise as him.

"Now I'm getting hungry. It's not easy whooping your ass all day." He smacked the table, letting me know the topic was moot.

I was hungry too. Then again, I was spoiled. Living with a chef will do that. Blake had been cooking up a storm lately. She said our kitchen was what she'd always imagined having when she had a home of her own. I was happy she liked it. I was going to gain a shit ton of weight.

"All right," I said. "Let's do this. I miss our girl anyway."

We pulled up at my brother's at the same time as the ladies. Three women piled out of Micah's car, but I only saw one. The hot-as-shit one carrying the white garment bag. I knew it wasn't like her to buy much. She hated shopping with a passion.

As I walked around my car, following Phil, I asked, "What did you buy me?"

An ear-to-ear smile reached across her pretty face.

"Well, I'll have you know, I bought my wedding dress today."

I knew they were *looking* for dresses, but I kind of thought those things took a little longer. I wasn't worried about her finding one, she'd look phenomenal in anything, but knowing the dress—*the dress*—was in that bag, well, it just hit home again that it was all real. And for the thousandth time in those few short weeks, I thanked God.

I approached and Micah said, "Hey, let's just leave all this stuff in the car. We'll come and get it later. Cory's about done with dinner." She took the dress from Blake and quickly hung it on the little doo-hickey in the backseat of her car.

"Yeah, your dad is starving." And I was too.

"Okay," she said. "Did you have fun?"

I wrapped my arm around her shoulders and walked her around the side of the house. "We had a good time. And you, for sure, without a doubt owe me."

She stopped. "Why? What happened?" Her tone was worried, but her expression wasn't too concerned.

"I told him about how we want the wedding. How it's going to be ours and that we're doing things a little differently and that you're walking solo."

Her face turned legitimately serious and she looked back at her parents, who were only a couple of feet behind us, and whispered, "What did he say?"

I kissed her forehead. I knew she'd been anxious about it,

and I was happy she didn't have to stress about it anymore.

"He was cool and said he only wants to see you happy. That it was *our* wedding and, ultimately, *our* choice how we did it."

Relief seemed to surround her and she kissed me. I know I'd bargained for a thank-you hummer, but I was satisfied with her thank-you kiss. It was sincere and it tasted like ease and contentment.

"Thank you, Casey. I love you."

Her imaginary debts were paid and I walked us to the fence door. Being the height I am, I saw it all before she did.

"Surprise!" sang through the air as the wooden door swung open in front of us.

It was both of our families, our friends, and our colleagues. And I laughed my ass off.

"You fuckers!" I accused. "And you!" I turned to her dad. "You were in on all of this?"

He only nodded and grinned.

"Holy shit," Blake said under her breath. "Look at all of this."

My brother's backyard looked like a hell-of-a-good time. Tables were set up with games and presents. Food was spread out on tables from one end to the other. Nearby was a photo booth. A sign hung on the back wall of the fence: *Congratulations, Blake and Casey.*

"I knew you were up to something," Blake accused Micah as she bound up with open arms.

"I know. We almost blew it. What do you think?"

"I don't know. I'm still a little stunned."

My brother came up behind his wife and wrapped an arm

around her waist as he kissed her cheek. "She's been planning this since the morning you guys called," he confessed.

Micah, the little sprite that she was, bounced on her toes. "It's an engagement—slash—couple's shower. Since you two set the date so quickly, there wasn't enough time for both. So I improvised." She waved an arm toward the backyard full of guests. "It's not much, but it's something to say we're so happy for you." She looked lovingly up into Cory's eyes and he smiled back at her. "We knew it was only a matter of time."

The party was one for the books. As I looked at her from across the yard, showing off her ring and retelling about how we got engaged, I couldn't really believe it. I mean, I believed it, but it was better than I'd imagined. Then I heard a familiar voice that put me in check.

Aly.

What in the living fuck was she doing there? Had they invited *her*? I pulled another Bay Brew from the cooler and spun to see if I was right. Of course, I was. Not three feet away, talking to my dad and Carmen, was Aly … and Nate?

And he had his arm around her?

And what the fuck?

I wasn't sure what to think. Aly was sly. She knew how to manipulate things. Situations. People. She wasn't my favorite person. Sure, I worked with her, but that's where my loyalty ended.

Nate noticed me about that time and nodded in my direction. It was a Friday night, so he must have made special arrangements to get off work at Hook, Line, and Sinker. I scanned the patio for Blake. I didn't want this to upset her, not after everything was going so well.

"Hey, man," Nate said and held his free hand out to shake. "Congratulations."

I took it and said, "Thanks," shaking my head to get my bearings.

Blake, as if I'd conjured her there, appeared at my side laying a silent, but very obvious, claim to me. Over the past few months, we'd both gotten used to touching in public. I know it sounds like a weird thing to admit, but when you're kind of not a thing, but really a *huge* thing, for over a couple of years—touching in front of people is a revelation. It's a claim. It's territorial. I knew all about that. Blake was mine. It wasn't a barbaric thing, it just was. My girl wanted everyone to see who I belonged to.

"Congratulations," Aly said—*to Blake.* I was skeptical. Honestly, I wanted to get the fuck out of there. It was awkward, to put it mildly.

"Thank you," Blake said politely. I knew she had a temper. I'd seen her temper and felt it in full force, but she had no reason to freak out. And she didn't. Her hand ran long lines up and down my back as she spoke, "And congratulations to you two. You look good together."

I know. You could probably imagine the sarcasm, but I shit you not, it wasn't there. It felt like a fucking episode of the Twilight Zone. My head swiveled to see Blake's face. Stoic and genuine, she stood there next to me like it was the most normal thing in the world.

Nate looked down at Aly and she gazed back up at him. The look was something private, and one that had nothing to do with us. Blake was right. They did look nice together. Happy even. Why hadn't I ever thought of that? Then again, I'd been a little preoccupied to play matchmaker.

Before I could filter myself, I misspoke, "You know she's bat-shit crazy, right?" Real smooth. I felt my fiancée pinch me in the back.

Aly looked a little embarrassed, but Nate didn't.

"I know," he smirked, not taking offense to my shitty timing. "But I like it."

I'll be a son-of-a-bitch. Had he always liked her? There was the time he almost beat my ass for being a dick to her after the violins tried to kill me. And the time after Cory's wedding when he allegedly drove her home after I ditched her. I didn't want to jump to conclusions, but that shit kind of added up.

Aly smiled. I still didn't trust the loon; she'd tricked me before. I worked with her, but since the time in my office when she'd assumed I was through with Blake and had to be corrected, she'd been professional. That was what … about eight months ago? Being an outside sales guy, I was rarely there. I hadn't seen her much at all.

I'd been busy and out of town. Then Blake was hurt and I was in Seattle for a few weeks. I hoped to God this wasn't a trick. I also hoped she didn't fuck with my bud. Nate was a great guy.

Then again, he was full-grown fucking man. He could take care of himself.

I must have looked like a psycho, I certainly sounded like one, but in the spirit of moving forward—Aly being there with Nate was perfect. I wasn't going to question it.

"I'll drink to crazy women," I said, trying to clean up my *faux pas* and I raised my bottle.

I wasn't about to stand around and beat a dead horse, so when Blake excused herself to introduce me to her bosses, I didn't hesitate to go with. As we walked over to where Lance and Bridgett were talking to Melanie, who worked with them, I asked her, "What do you think of that?" I rolled my eyes back to Nate and the possibly reformed head-case I'd once dated.

"I think it's great," she said easily.

"You do?" Where was my Blake and who was this by-gone-tolerant saint?

"I do. Nobody's perfect. I've made my fair share of mis-takes and done some pretty idiotic things. It's nice to see her with someone who seems to accept all that." She grabbed my hand and we walked. "Plus, now she might leave my man the fuck alone."

Have I ever mentioned how much I love it when she said fuck? I'm sure I have. Something about that pretty little mouth saying something so off-color. Like when a child says it and it's cute, or something. Sure, she was trying to be bad-ass, and I'd pretend she totally was, but her swearing had the opposite effect on me. It made her more endearing.

The party lasted late into the night. Most of our co-workers left early, but our family pretty much hung out until we decided it was time to call a cab. Funny how just last year any mention of what was going on with Blake and me was cause for argument, and now I laughed when they made fun of how whipped I was. Had *always* been.

And, best of all, we were getting fucking married.

FIFTEEN

Blake

Saturday, August 7, 2010

"WE'RE GOING TO GET so married, Casey," I said. I was drunk so it probably didn't sound like that. Not to mention on the way home from our engagement/couple's shower, I told him about thirty times. I couldn't stop myself.

"I know," he insisted. "You told me."

"But I don't think you get it. I'm marrying *you*. You're so hot and fun and *hot*." Did I say hot twice? Well that was fine, because he was two times the hotness anyway. I lay my head on his lap as the taxi drove us home. The streetlights made everything so blurry.

Bright. Dim. Bright. Dim. It was making everything spin.

"That's a lot of hot. You know I'm not just a pretty face, right?" He looked down at me and grinned just like the time he told me I was trouble at Hook, Line, and Sinker.

Why didn't he sound as drunk as me?

I closed my eyes. Those fucking pole lights were tempting my stomach.

"I know. You've also got a great co—" Then my mouth was covered and I felt the rumble of him laughing against my ear.

"We should talk about this when we get home," he suggested quietly. "We don't want the driver to get jealous."

That was a good point. Maybe the car driver had a tiny penis. Casey was so thoughtful. Always thinking about others.

"You're so sweet. I love you."

I felt the car go over the hump in our driveway and slow to a stop. Casey leaned over my face and handed the guy money.

"Thanks, I'm going to get her to bed," he told him.

I lifted up on my own, and the whole car did a three sixty-nine. Or a thirty-six. Or whatever. The car spun around. Casey opened his door and held a hand out to me. I think he was dicking with me because it took two tries for me to get it. Doesn't he know it's not polite to mess with drunk people?

I got out of the cab okay, but I did not stand up okay. My ankle twisted, probably because I wasn't wearing cocktail-safe shoes. So I tried to sit back down in the car; I could walk if I took those damn shoes off.

"Oh, no you don't." Casey picked me up before my ass hit

the seat.

"I can walk. These shoes aren't working."

"I've got you. Let's just get inside before you start stripping. Then you can take off whatever you want."

"I'm not a stripper-er. I'm a chef. Well, I was. Now I'm just a person on her computer who talks to chefs."

He unlocked the front door, with me in his arms, and kicked it shut behind us. He plopped me down on the couch in the living room and squatted down to work on my heels.

"Do you miss cooking at work?" He slipped off the first and began working on the second. I swayed side to side as I watched. My fiancé always took such good care of me.

"Yeah, I like doing it myself. I like when people like *my* food. Not just food I told them to make, Casey. The food *I* made. Myself."

He sat completely down on the rug and then I thought I was going to die. He held my left foot—or was it my right foot—in his hands and worked them over. His thumbs pressing into the achy soles of my feet.

"Shit. That feels good."

I heard him laugh at me, but I didn't care. I lay back into the soft couch and relished the feeling of his fingers as they masterfully squeezed and kneaded me in the most delicious way.

"Well, can you do more of that at work?"

"No. They don't need me for that. They have chefs for that. I'm thirsty."

"You know what? That's not a bad idea. You need some Gatorade. Can you make it to the bedroom? I'll get drinks and some stuff for the headache you'll most definitely have in the morning."

My feet felt better and the spinning had come to a stop since we weren't in the car anymore. "Yeah, I'm cool. I'm gonna go to bed."

As I walked down the hall to our room, I kicked off my skirt and flung it into the hamper … and made a basket. From like a hundred feet away.

Why isn't anyone ever around when I do that?

I took my shirt off and stood in the same spot. Going for two.

I shot.

I missed.

"So close," he said from behind me.

"No, you didn't see it. I just made it."

He gently swatted my ass as he passed me. "You made it on the floor, Betty Ford."

"Uh," I protested and followed him. Nobody would ever know how good I was.

"Want a T-shirt?" he asked, placing a bunch of goodies on my nightstand. Two cheese sticks—because he knew better than to just bring one, that little episode was almost our first domestic fight—a stem of grapes, a pack of cheese and peanut butter crackers, and the promised Gatorade.

"Yes, please." I climbed into bed. I'd wait for him to get back before I dug in. I laid my head on my pillow and watched as he went into the bathroom, kicked off his shoes, and took his jeans off.

My eyes got heavy and I tried to keep them open, but I failed.

I awoke to the sound of Casey talking, but it wasn't to me. When my ears started processing English, I caught him saying, "She's still asleep. I'm not waking her up. I'd like to actually live to see my wedding day, Morgan." That made me smile. It was then I realized smiling kind of hurt. I rolled over and climbed to the end of the bed to hear more clearly. It wasn't eavesdropping though. I lived there. If he didn't want me to hear something, he'd have to figure something else out.

"I think she'll be fine. She didn't throw up or anything." Then he paused and laughed. "I know. I didn't realize they were that competitive either. I agree, Reggie got the better-at-beer-games genes."

That offended me. Well, kind of.

"Hey, I can hear you," I called. "And I was just having an off night."

I heard his bare feet slap across the floor down the hall. "Well, you better pray you don't have one tonight."

"Why?"

"Because I was just informed, by a bossy brat, that tonight is your bachelorette party."

I slung an arm over my face. The thought of drinking didn't appeal to me and it made my tummy grumble. Or maybe I was just hungry.

He sat next to me on the bed and rubbed my boob. I mouthed

You're on the phone with your sister. Stop. That's gross.

He mouthed *I'll show you gross.*

I giggled into the mattress. He was so warped. I worried about his mental health sometimes.

I couldn't hear what she was saying, but she was letting him have it. She was always letting him have it. I was really beginning to love her for that. She didn't take his shit and he took *all* of hers.

"I said I would, okay? Now what time?" he asked, annoyed and ready to get off the phone. His hand had already wandered between my legs. He was a great multitasker. "Okay, bye. Okay! I will. Love you too."

"Bachelorette party?" My head swam. I was starving. I needed a shower and most importantly, I was desperate for coffee.

"They're picking you up at seven." He lay down next to me, but I feared for his health if he got much closer. I was fairly positive my breath could peel paint. I brought the sheet up to my mouth to spare him.

"What time is it now?" I asked through the linen.

"It's only nine. You have plenty of time to bleach your mouth out and knock off the big chunks in the shower." *Why wasn't he hungover?* I'm sure he drank more than I had.

"How do you feel?" I asked. He appeared fresh as a fucking spring lamb. It was kind of bullshit.

"I'm great. Plus, a package arrived for you."

I clumsily thumbed through my mind trying to remember what I'd ordered. I came up short. "I don't think I ordered anything."

"You didn't. I did. It's actually a few packages."

"You have my attention."

We were never big on gifts. In fact, we'd never exchanged gifts for holidays or birthdays. I knew his birthday was right before Christmas—only through Micah had I learned that. I was always too afraid to buy him things, because I didn't want him to buy me things that would make me miss him. That was before. Before I got my shit together. Before the wakeup call. Before my divorce and our engagement. We'd officially made it past the shitty *before* phase we'd blocked ourselves into.

Suddenly, I didn't feel that bad. I would survive. At least long enough to open up my presents.

"I have coffee and Pop-Tarts waiting for you in the kitchen."

Like the perfect example of grace and agility, I kicked my legs free of the tangled sheet and damn near fell off the bed.

"You're a beautiful mess today," he teased.

"Why, thank you."

"It's a fucking bike!" I shouted as I tore the cardboard off the humongous box. Well, it might be a bike. At the moment it was just bars and wheels and some other stuff in a box. "You bought me a bike?"

"Yeah, I have a lot of special days to make up for. Plus, it's kind of for me too. I miss riding, but I want you to come with me."

"Will you help me put it together?" I was smart. I was competent. What I was not, was industrious. In theory, I could put things together. I understood directions, but implementing them and getting them right? Well, I'm a big enough girl to admit I could use some help.

"You bet your sweet ass I will." He showed me the wrench he already had in his back pocket. Casey with tools. Totally hot. "I'll slap this together while you shower, and if everything else fits, we'll go for our maiden voyage."

Fits? I was lost.

He walked to the closet by the front door and pulled out two big gift bags. If I wasn't so excited I may have felt bad for not having anything to give him.

"All of this is mine, too?"

"Oh, yeah," he scoffed. "Any girl of mine has to have her own gear." He handed me bags from a sporting goods store and sat on the arm of the couch as I began pulling things out.

A helmet, gloves, knee and elbow pads, a sports bra and tiny riding shorts, new sunglasses, sweat bands, a cool water bottle, a fun handle-bar bell thingy, an iPod pouch for my arm, shoes and socks—he'd thought of it all. It was thoughtful and just like him. The only tiny problem was all of it matched. Like *really* matched.

No doubt, he hadn't any help from his sisters.

The thing is—yes, women like things to coordinate, but everything was purple and yellow. I was going to look like a bike-riding misfit superhero.

It didn't matter though. He'd bought it so we could do something he loved together. I'd just have to tolerate looking like goober-grape the bicycle safety queen. And wasn't that a gift … for him? Maybe the idea was a stretch, but it was with some deep breaths and a full cup of coffee that I prepared myself to look like a real dork in the name of love.

I showered while he put my bike together and laughed at myself in the mirror afterward for a good five minutes.

Dressed from head to toe in Casey's *gifts*, I found him airing the tires in the garage.

"Ah! Hahahaha," he erupted. "You look ridiculous." He had to turn away to get a grip. I looked down at myself and silently agreed.

"It's not *that* bad."

"It's not? You look like the result of a purple and yellow crayon gang war. It looks like a costume." He could barely choke out his words between his attempts to breathe. "Do you want to wear it? It won't hurt my feelings if you take some of it off."

I didn't want to take any of it off. As dumb as I looked and felt, I was proud of my present. Thank God the bike was a nice silver color. Had it been either purple or yellow too, I would have pretended to be much more hungover.

"Nope, I'm wearing it and you have to ride with me," I said, turning the embarrassment back at him. We'd have to share this humiliation.

He quirked an eyebrow like I'd challenged him. "Okay then, I'll go get my shoes on."

While I waited, I straddled my bike. It was actually really comfortable. I bargained with the universe that since I was wearing the most atrocious riding outfit, they'd let me not wreck on our first ride. It was going to be a challenge to pull cool off, but I'd give it my best shot.

Soon Casey came out of the laundry room door and I fell purple-helmet-head-over-yellow-sneakers in love with him all over again. He wore a midriff cut-off Frankie Says Relax T-shirt, the shortest pair of running shorts I'd ever seen, a lime-green headband, blue aviators, and a very well kept vintage pair of Air Jordan's, laced up the cool way—tongues out.

"Honeybee," he shouted with gusto and clapped his hands together. "Let's ride."

Some men would have told me to change. Some men wouldn't have put in the effort—or thought—into buying the array of thoughtful accessories he had. Some men would have gone into the house and put on typical riding clothes.

Not my man. He embraced it and instead of us being a weirdo and a hot guy out for a ride, we were a *pair* of weirdos in love.

SIXTEEN

Casey

Saturday, August 7, 2010

MY GIRL WAS A beast and we looked like two fools in love.

Not only did she not whine and complain about the crazy things I'd bought for her to wear—and in my defense, I didn't imagine it looking like *that*—but she seemed to really enjoy it. We didn't go anywhere too extreme for our first ride, but I wanted to show her a few of my favorite spots. Our house was in a great location for riding no matter what your skill level. We took the road that went up the back of a small bluff overlooking the bay. I'd packed a few things in the small pouch on my bike and we stopped to catch our breath and get a drink.

I checked my phone for the time and saw I had a message from Cory.

Cory: I hope you're ready for tonight, bro. You're getting torn up bachelor-style. We'll be there at 7:30 for pre-game.

I'd suspected as much. And to their credit, it worked out really great since everyone was in town. Blake's family was staying at the Ashcroft Hotel downtown, the same one we'd had our first night in, and Troy was crashing at Cory and Micah's. Audrey was at my dad and Carmen's, where Morgan still lived. To be quite honest, I loved knowing that our family was all in one place. Our wedding was going to be a lot of fun.

Me: I'll be ready. I'm always ready to drink you under the table.

"So how's that new bike treating you? You doing okay?" It wasn't my style to worry and fret over someone, but that woman's body had been through the wringer, and not that long ago. I watched as she drank water, some of it spilling down the front of her, and thanked God that she hadn't been hurt worse. Fuck, the way she fell, she could have very easily been paralyzed. She could have broken her back or neck. At the very least, she could have broken an arm or leg. Sure her injuries were fucking awful, but her healing as fast as she did helped me stay sane and thankful they weren't worse.

"I feel great. My leg muscles burn, but I'm pretty good I think."

I'd worked up a good sweat on the way up and so had she. It was running down her forehead from under her helmet.

"Are you hot in that thing?" I'd bought it only because when we'd talked about it before, she'd said she wasn't that good. I thought she was doing fine, but I especially liked knowing her pretty little melon was safer while we rode. Even if I didn't wear one. I also didn't wear the knee or elbow guards like I'd bought for her. She looked hilarious, but still gorgeous as hell. Despite the purple and yellow travesty I'd given her.

"Actually, I forgot it was on." She unlatched it from the bottom and shook out her hair. "Whoa, that does feel cooler though." I took it from her and fastened it to the bar under her seat. She didn't have to wear it if she felt confident. I simply didn't want her to get hurt.

"I guess I went a little overboard with the matching."

"It's okay. You just care, Lou." She pulled her phone from the armband. "Come here. Let's take a picture."

We turned around so both our bikes and the bay were in the shot and I took the picture for us. After I took a *good* one, she kissed me on my cheek.

"I love you. Thanks for my new ride."

"You're welcome. Anytime."

It was going to be so fucking fun spoiling her for the rest of our lives.

"Have fun and be careful," I told her as I kissed her by the front door when the girls picked her up. "Call me if you need anything."

"Oh, I'm sure you won't be able to do anything about it. My brothers and your brother are going to get you wasted," she insisted. "No hookers. No drugs. No jail time." Those were pretty decent rules. Surely, I could keep my night within her boundaries. Especially since I'd never been with a hooker, never was much for drugs, and had a clean legal record. So far.

"You too. No swallowing. No tattoos without me. And no leaving the country." She wasn't a flight risk like she used to be, but for clarity's sake, it needed to be mentioned.

And fuck did she look good. Hot-ass little black dress, a second night in a row wearing shoes that weren't fit for drinking in, and her face was the picture of happiness.

"On second thought," I added and opened the closet for what I needed, "you better just wear this tonight too." When she saw it was the purple helmet, she gave me a look only a man could translate. It said, *don't even fucking think about it, Casey Moore*.

"Ha, no way in hell."

I kissed her one last time, not giving a shit about the lipstick I'd, no doubt, have to go scrub off. I had time and besides, it was totally worth it.

"Go have fun," I said just as the girls in the car became impatient and honked.

"Okay, be careful. I'll see you later."

I watched her cute ass walk away as I waved at those responsible for showing my favorite girl a good time. The women in that car would take care of her. I didn't have to worry. Morgan was there, after all. *Ms. Sense and Sensibility.*

I was looking forward to a guys' night out. It was a very safe bet we weren't going to a strip club, being that Blake's two older brothers were along for the ride. I didn't expect either of them would want to go out to the clubs. Then again, Shane, Reggie, and Troy were all single.

Fuck, I didn't know what I was getting into. Some things never changed.

"This is a really nice place, man," Shane said, taking a look at our home. It was actually beginning to feel like ours too. Little by little we were making it less like my mother's and more like Casey and Blake's. Truthfully, Blake had done a lot.

"Thanks, we love it here."

"You guys grew up in this house, right?" he asked, as he walked around looking at the fireplace and the view out back. "This would have been a fun place to grow up."

"We did. It was." I looked out the back with him. I could remember playing outside until it was dark. The treehouse my dad had built on the edge of the woods was still standing, even though it could use a little work. It hit me that I'd be able to fix it up one day for our kids. The garden would never die and the shed would probably never need to be painted again.

"So are you ready?" he asked.

"Yeah, I've got some cold beers if you'd like one and then we can head to wherever the hell it is you guys are taking me."

"No, I mean about being married."

Now I'd only met Shane a few times; I was much more familiar with Reggie. We hadn't had much time to shoot the shit. From what I knew about him, he was pretty laid-back, and for the past few months, he'd been doing better since his divorce a year or so ago. Of course, all of this information was second-hand from Blake.

I tipped back my beer and thought about what he'd asked. Was I ready? It didn't take long to land on the only answer that felt right.

"Am I afraid I won't make her happy enough? Sometimes. Am I ready to do every fucking thing in my power to see that she is? You're damn right. We've been waiting for this, or hoping for it really, for a long time. Blake's the one for me." I looked him in the eye. He didn't have the aggressive aura about him like Reggie though. His was a quiet type. He'd been there. He'd had a wife. And, as shitty as it was, it didn't last.

So having him ask me if I was ready almost felt more like a warning, because he'd probably be able to see if shit was heading south. It was my job to make sure it didn't.

"Good. She's a good girl. She keeps a lot of things to herself, like I do. I know you probably don't see that side of her, but it's in there. Just make sure you're always looking for what she's *trying* to tell you. If I know anything, it's all about not hearing what a woman was saying." He chuckled. "Hell, mine was telling me she wasn't happy for a long time. Probably before we ever got married."

"Well, I'm not saying Blake always tells me what's on her mind, but I'd like to think somehow she lets me know when she needs me. Does that make sense?" Shit was getting deep. I thought this night was supposed to be about being wild and taking things to excess. So far it was just five dudes at my house having a beer and talking about relationships.

We were getting fucking old.

"Well, as long as she's happy. Now where's this beer you promised me?"

And that was that. I liked his approach. Honest. Direct. And most importantly, brief.

"Ok, pussy," Troy announced. "How much cash do you have on ya?" That didn't sound good.

I think I had about five hundred in my wallet.

"Enough, why?"

"Because you're going to lose it all tonight."

This was going to get ugly. I could feel it.

After we hung out for a few hours and smoked a couple cigars Reggie had brought for the occasion, we headed out. Back in the days before I met Blake, I wouldn't think twice about going to a strip club. Dancers aren't really my cup of tea, but I got it. I loved looking at women, and lap dances weren't torture, but

I didn't have it in me anymore. When we pulled up to a gentlemen's club I'd heard of, I will admit, I thought about saying fuck it and suggesting we just go shoot darts at HLS.

"Guys, are you sure about this?" I asked as we got out of Cory's SUV. "I'm up for having some fun, but really? Strip club? You couldn't think of anything else?"

I watched as knowing looks swept across their faces. There was something going on.

Cory, my always sure-headed, older-by-a-few-minutes brother, draped an arm over my shoulder and started walking us across the street. He said, "Listen, we're going to go in, we'll have a few drinks, and go up to a private room to play some poker."

Fuck if I wasn't whipped, because I sure as hell felt better knowing I wasn't going to be swarmed with naked women in front of my soon to be in-laws. And I *love* tits. I felt a little better and surrendered, because I was in good hands.

Strip club it was.

The Elite wasn't a typical club. There were no visible tables from the entrance. The bar looked and felt like one of the more upscale bars I'd ever been in. The wait staff was definitely dressed better than any I'd ever seen, wearing short dresses that did a fantastic job of adding to the allure. As women walked past us, they smiled coyly. I'm only a man, so I smiled back.

Reggie walked up to a guy in a suit, who he must have known. They shook hands and laughed and then the guy looked right at me, nodding. I was being fooled. This was just a high-end booby trap. Suit guy motioned to one of the ladies who walked over to us.

"Are you Mr. Moore?" Her tone was very inviting.

"Well, I'm one of them," I answered. She looked a little confused, but right away noticed Cory.

"Oh, twins. My favorite." Whoa. That was one thing I'd never done.

She linked her arm with mine and led me away. My entourage followed. It was kind of cool. She wasn't trying to paw at me, which was nice. She was attractive, but it wasn't hard to tell she was wearing a pretty dress her ass hung out of for the sole purpose of making money.

To me that seemed a little sad. A little desperate. The only brand of desperate I was into was when Blake was reaching for an orgasm.

Shit. I needed to watch what I was thinking about or I'd get a memory boner. Although, the thought of Blake wearing something like that, and prancing me around on her arm up to some private location … well, I could definitely work that into some alone time in the future, if needed. In fact, I'd tell her about this new little fantasy and see what happened.

Squeaky wheel gets the grease, right?

We went up a lengthy staircase that led into a huge room. There was a private bar and a very nice poker table waiting for us. Cory wasn't lying and that's why I needed money. Troy, the fucker, was trying to rob me on my night. I'd have to teach him a lesson. I'm a fucking salesman. I could sell ketchup popsicles to a nun in white gloves—with a straight face. I was going to make him my bitch just for doubting me.

"Gentlemen, I'm Curtis. I'll be your dealer tonight." Curtis was an older man, but he looked like he could still get into some trouble. He had that tangerine George Hamilton glow. "Help yourselves to the bar, and we'll get started whenever you're ready. We also have ladies available, in the event you lose and need some consolation and ego stroking."

If that wasn't some innuendo.

It was a special occasion, so I ordered off the top shelf. Rémy Martin neat.

Honeybee.

I hoped Blake was enjoying herself. If I needed some guy time, she sure as hell needed a girls' night out.

All five of us sat around the pristine green-felt table and Curtis began to shuffle.

"The game is Texas Hold 'Em. Ten and twenty-dollar blinds. Who's in and who's out? Ante up."

For the first time in my life, I felt like I couldn't lose.

SEVENTEEN

Blake

Saturday, August 7, 2010

AT FIRST, I THOUGHT they'd lost their minds, but we were having so much fun. Somehow they'd arranged a private showing of lingerie at a swanky shop called Madame Amour's downtown. I wasn't too hip on strutting around in anything too risky in front of Casey's little sisters, but they felt more like my friends now. Besides, even Morgan was on board and having a good time.

"Do you see anything you like?" she asked me. "Or better yet—as weird as it sounds—see anything Casey would like?

Never mind." Then she walked away, shaking out her hee-bee-jeebees.

Well, at least she was trying.

There were lots of things he would like. One of everything in the place I was certain. I had the honeymoon—which I didn't know much about—to buy for, as well as our wedding night.

"Another champagne?" our attendant Gwen asked.

"Yes, please."

"Me too," added Melanie, my co-worker, and Micah in unison. I was enjoying the girl time, and kind of glad the mothers stayed behind to watch Foster.

"Try some of it on," Melanie said. "That's what we're here for. I'm going to before we eat."

Micah had already tried three or four things on, admitting Cory gave her the credit card and took away her monthly limit. She wasn't holding back with the stack she'd already decided to purchase.

"Okay, I'm going in." Once again, I was in a dressing room, a familiar place when you're actually *into* planning a wedding. The first few things I tried on were nos from me. However, I'd lay money Casey would come in his pants if I sent him a snapshot of me in the dressing room. I saved that idea for when I found one I liked. The first one that caught my eye was a slutty little red number with barely enough fabric to be classified as clothing. It was more like jewelry. A little swatch of satin here, a scrap of lace there. I snapped a quick picture and moved to the next.

I loved it. I was glad it had a little instruction tag on how to put in on. It was basically just one long, thick, black silk ribbon.

You wound it around parts and then it tied around the front in a chic bow. Surprisingly, it covered a lot and stayed where it was intended. Plus, it was super comfortable and I kind of felt like cat woman.

I decided on both of those and a few new bras and panties. I bought two wedding garters, one to keep and one to throw. The night wasn't all about kinky fun, as it also allowed me to check a few things off my list. Bonus.

They catered in an elegant, yet light dinner of blackened salmon and spring-mix salads. We dined together, laughing about the lingerie mishaps we'd all encountered. The champagne never dried up and our glasses were never empty. For dessert it was hot-fudgey chocolate and strawberries.

"So are you ready for our next stop?" Audrey asked with a secret hidden in her smile, just like Casey's.

"Next stop? I thought this was the party." I looked around from Morgan to Melanie to Micah. None of them were saying anything. "Well, it looks like I don't really have a choice. Now do I?"

"Nope," Audrey giggled. I was in for it.

The bitches blindfolded me. It was bad enough they weren't telling me where we were going, but they wouldn't even let me see. I'd never been blindfolded before, but in the back of my head I was thinking I'd be keeping it. You never know when a little blindfold might come in handy. Especially when you were bringing home half a grand in sexy lingerie.

I listened to the sounds around us, but I didn't recognize anything more than a busy Saturday night in the city. When we came to a stop, Audrey helped me out and she and Morgan looped my arms through theirs. They walked slowly with me and I appreciated it. I was wearing dangerous shoes and I didn't really like the thought of falling down. Plus, I'd had a good amount to drink already.

"Okay, step," Morgan instructed. "Again. Again."

"Okay, just tell me when *not* to step." She laughed and agreed.

I heard Melanie whisper, I'm assuming to Micah, "She's going to kill us." That didn't make me feel very confident.

I heard a lot of bass, but it sounded like it was on the other side of a wall. The stairway seemed to go on and on forever. Finally, at the top there was a voice I didn't recognize. It was a woman's.

"Welcome, ladies. I see you have our special guest with you." Her accent wasn't too thick to understand, but it was definitely German, or Swedish, or something like that. "Please, walk her this way and we'll show her what we have in store."

I heard more music, but it wasn't the same as from before. This was quieter.

My senses were working overtime. I smelled cigars and perfume. The sounds of everyone's heels clicking and clacking across a wooden floor.

"Okay, Miss Bride-to-be, are you ready for a lesson?"

A lesson? In what? Romance languages?

The blindfold was ripped off my head and in front of me were ten shiny brass poles.

Shit.

It was a pole dancing class. They were trying to teach me how to be a stripper? I guessed that was better than taking me to *see* strippers. Especially the greasy male ones.

"So, what do you think?" she asked. I found her voice off to the side and took inventory of who would be our instructor. She was lean, beautiful, probably about forty, but the muscles on that woman were warning enough not to cross her. She could seriously kick my ass.

Micah walked up with two glasses of bubbly.

"Fuck it. Let's do this. Teach me the ways." I downed my glass. My ladylike sensibilities gone. I'd consumed just enough to drink and felt adventurous enough to give it a shot.

"My name is Sabrina, and I'll teach you how to work your body, show off your confidence and drive your lover mad." Maybe I was drunk, but I was kind of buying it. The way she popped her hip when she listed what she planned. If she really thought she could do that in a few hours, I might as well give it a shot. "Who is Mee-ka?" she asked.

I liked the way she spoke. I figured if the pole dancing part fell through, I could at least try to talk like her in the bedroom. Then I laughed at the thought a little louder than I should have and Morgan elbowed me.

"I'm Micah."

"Did you bring the outfits?"

Outfits? It just kept getting better and better.

"Yup, they're right here," she answered like a straight-up teacher's pet. Then again, if Sabrina told me to hang upside down from the ceiling, I'd figure out a way. She meant business.

"Per-feect! Now, ladies, please excuse yourselves to change. I will wait right here." None of us moved. She clapped twice. Loud and fast. "Chop. Chop."

When Micah handed what I was expecting to be gym sweats and a sports bra, I started looking for a window. It was the ribbon get up from the boutique.

"You've got to be out of your fucking mind if you think I'm getting in this and riding a pole," I informed her. "I can't do it."

"Yes, you can. It'll be fun. We're all doing it. And look. I knew you'd freak out, so I got the same one. We're like sexy twins."

"Ha!" exclaimed Audrey. "Just like our brothers always *thought* they were."

When I saw that even Morgan was wearing a baby-doll nightshirt and lacy boy shorts, I knew there was no backing out. If she was doing it, I had to.

"Now chug this and suit up," Melanie said and handed me her glass.

It wasn't so bad, like they said. We were all doing it and so that made it a lot less embarrassing. Sabrina let us start with our shoes off, since she didn't want us to impale ourselves right off the bat. Some of what she did looked so easy, but she explained it was because she wasn't afraid of it.

"There is no room for fear in confidence. The pole is sexy. Yes? The clothes are sexy. Yes? The woman is sexy. Yes? She knows what her lover likes. It is in her posture. It is in her walk.

It is in her eyes. You do all of this, the pole means nothing." She had a point.

We were all facing ourselves in the mirrors that lined the wall and she had us practice walking around the pole with our backs straight, heads up. She might be crazy, but it *was* sexier. My body looked like it knew what it was doing.

Maybe I could fake this shit?

The music grew louder which allowed us to focus on how we were moving more. All of the songs were seductive and sensual. She added a few moves that were more about using the pole as support. A seductive bend in front of it. A low dip to the floor and using it to stay balanced on your way back up. A long stretch with our hands above our heads, coupled with a naughty ass-shake. She even showed us a little twirl that, to my surprise, wasn't too damn hard after I got the feel of it. Not only was it a fantastic workout, but it was so much fun. Laughing and drinking with my favorite girls. Being silly and doing something none of us had ever done before.

I also thought, Casey would lose his mind if I had one installed somewhere in the house. That would be a nice thank you for my bike.

It was decidedly the best bachelorette party in history. I didn't even have one—you know—before.

"Ok, ladies. Where did we put the lovely blindfold? It is time for her surprise."

Another surprise? I was almost exhausted. I was hoping for cake and some water. I didn't mean to be a spoilsport, but after the ride we went on earlier and wearing the shoes and doing all the dancing—well, it took it out of this pretend first-time exotic dancer.

On went the blindfold, but I just went with it. I didn't know what was going to happen, but I had trust I was in good hands. My girls really kicked ass.

EIGHTEEN

Casey

Saturday, August 7, 2010

I WAS KICKING ASS.

I hadn't planned on getting *that* into the game, but it was only Reggie and me left and there was a shit load of money on the table.

"Okay, let's up it a little?" he asked before the dealer started to deal out the last hand, unless we both busted. The drinks were going down smooth and the cigars were even smoother. The haze in the room only parted when one of the half-naked wait staff passed by. I was glad they hadn't wanted to go to a *real* strip club. That just felt weird.

But then Reggie had to go and bring it all back up.

"Loser gets a dance with a girl in the private room."

My head immediately shook. That wasn't going to happen. Then again, he was an impressive player. There was a really good chance he was about to win it all. And if I lost, I did not want to have a private dance with a stripper.

What was he thinking? I was marrying his sister for fuck's sake.

"That's not a good idea. Reggie, come on. I'm about to get married to the woman of my dreams. I don't need a dance. Let's just play and winner takes the cash." I didn't give a shit about the money. I gave a shit about my word to Blake. Strippers weren't really cheating, but it was gray territory. And I didn't want to wander into it.

"Okay, you win, you take the cash. I win, you take the cash *and* get the dance." If I'd needed the money that was a good fucking bet to take. Only, if I lost I had to do the private dance shit.

Troy and Shane had already had two private dances apiece. Troy leaned over my shoulder and said, "Dude, you have nothing to worry about. They don't even touch you. It sucks."

It still didn't feel right. I looked over at her other brother, Shane. He'd tell me the truth.

"He's right. It was pretty tame, Casey. You're fine. Nothing to worry about."

"So are you in?" Curtis asked.

I looked around the room at these guys. Guys who I trusted, and thought, to hell with it. I'm at my bachelor party. I knew how protective they were of their sister. If it would hurt her, they would have no part of it.

"Deal me in," I resigned. "I'm going to kick your ass."

He laughed pretty hard. "Damn, dude. I've never seen a man so afraid of a lap dance before."

I got a six and a four.

He got a nine and a Jack.

The dealer flopped eight, nine, Ace.

The turn was a four.

At least I had a chance. I needed another four or a six.

The river came out a Queen.

I was getting a lap dance.

Fuck.

I was led off to a small room on the other side of the area where we'd been playing poker. I was glad for not having to walk through the club with a girl. I still had a sinking feeling in my gut.

Honeybee, I'll pretend it's you. I swear. Wait. Then I'll get hard. Fuck.

I heard Reggie say when I was just about to go in, "Don't worry, man. I think I'm going to get one too anyway. When in Rome …" Then he laughed his ass off at my expense.

The private room was in the shape of a half circle. The

curved wall was made of a mirror and there was a pole just a few feet away from it. Maybe they were right. Pole dancers weren't *exactly* strippers. What was odd was there wasn't a whole lot of room between the pole and the wall, possibly only three feet. I supposed it was enough for what the room was intended.

I didn't want to overthink it. Hopefully it would just be a nice performance. A short. Tame. Performance.

The blonde who walked me to the private room led me toward an armless chair. I sat. The sooner this was over, the sooner I could get back home to Blake. I hoped she was having fun. The girl punched a few things on a keypad on the wall. The lights dimmed and music started.

She knocked twice on the other wall.

"Enjoy," she said and left the way we came in. The lights were low, casting a sensual glow and I looked at my reflection.

What am I doing here?

The wall opened in the center and the door curved out. I saw a tall woman. She was older than me, but she was in seriously better shape. She could have probably bench-pressed me.

"Hello, I'm Sabrina. I'm here to secure you to your chair … for your safety."

My safety? Yeah, okay.

With two straps of silk, she gathered my hands behind the chair. It was comfortable and the knots weren't too tight. I could get away if shit started to get rough. And I'm not lying. She looked like she could hold her own and spoke like a sexy version of a Swiss-army pole dancer.

"Now that you are comfortable, I'll be back with your dancer." She was only gone a minute before she came back with a woman wearing a blindfold.

It was *my* woman in a blindfold.

My woman wearing some kind of lingerie *and* a blindfold.

Fucking fuck of all fucks. She. Was. *Hot.*

Sabrina the stripper sergeant raised one finger over her mouth to tell me to be quiet.

"Where are we going?" Blake asked. Her head tilted up in question not being able to tell where she was. "Is this the dressing room?"

"Take your time, Miss Bride-to-be. Remember what I taught you." She walked Blake just inside and then left, closing the door with a click.

Now that was more like it. Blake didn't know if she was alone or not. She turned her head toward the sound of the door latching behind her. The music got gradually louder.

"Hello?" she asked into the dim room. Then she removed the blindfold, blinking her sight back into focus. When she saw me her hand covered her laugh. She'd had a few drinks. Quite a few if she got into that get up without a fight. Then again, Sabrina didn't look like she took much shit. However, that woman said something which had my attention.

What had she *taught* her?

"Are you tied up?" Blake asked, seeing my hands behind my back.

"I was tricked," I confessed.

"Oh, you were?" she said skeptically, but the humor in her eyes gave me relief. Her being there in general relieved me, but knowing she was having fun—just by her expression—made all of my earlier protesting hilarious. "Were you expecting a professional?"

"I didn't know what to expect. I lost a bet."

She nodded in understanding.

"I think they set us up."

"I think you're right."

Set up or not, there we were. My fiancée was half-naked and I was tied to a chair.

After the shock started to wear off, I asked what was really on my mind. "What did she show you, Blake?"

Blake faked Sabrina's accent and said, "How to seduce my loverrrr."

"Well, I'm right here. Seduce away."

I didn't know whether to hate the dudes I came with or if I owed them anything they wanted. Looking at the situation, I'd say I owed them. Big time.

She swayed a little, either from the drinks she'd had or she was just finding her rhythm. Her hips rocked side to side. I quickly learned it was both. As she began to walk around the pole, letting it hold her weight as she twirled, I watched her chest jump.

My pole dancer had hiccups.

Sexiest fucking hiccups I'd ever seen.

The bass thumped and she kept time like she actually knew what she was doing. Her posture was straight as an arrow and her legs spread wide, as she slid almost all the way to the floor. Seductively, she surveyed me studying her. As I watched, she bloomed into a full-on sex goddess before my very eyes. Dipping a finger in her mouth, then slowly running it down the center of her chest, all the way to her barely hidden pussy. She clearly liked my reaction—shifting in my seat—because she repeated the act until she had both hands on her center. I almost came unglued when she rubbed herself through the black fabric as she stood confidently before me. Then she turned and grabbed the pole with one hand, bending at the hip as she shoved her ass close to my face.

I licked my lips. I wanted untied. I needed untied.

Her hand lingered on the spot I craved more than ever, then slid back, and she tapped her pussy in front of my face. Her ass hypnotically moved back and forth in front of me. When she turned back around and we were face to face, with one little finger she pushed me back in my seat. Then she hopped up on the pole and I'll be damned if she didn't spin on the son of a bitch. I was wrong. There was plenty of room for a naughty twirl.

I've had hard-ons before. Lots of them. I've never had one like that. It was uncomfortable. It was persistent and about to break through my pants—Hulk style. It was getting angry for being so neglected.

"Honeybee," I pleaded. "Untie me."

The tease pretended to think about it.

Showing mercy, she straddled me. That was better.

"I'm not sure you want to be untied. Feels like you're enjoying yourself." Her sweet breath was like a narcotic to my senses.

Our mouths crashed into each other. Her tongue led mine in a seductive dance, rivaling the show I'd witnessed. My girl had skills. I couldn't wait to talk to her about her night. But at the moment, I was enjoying the whole private room experience.

With her still moving to the music and her weight on my

already swollen cock, she had hell turning into heaven in that one kiss.

We could do whatever we wanted. They weren't likely to bother us after setting this up.

"Untie me, please," I requested again into her mouth. "I promise to tip for the extras."

She laughed, but making her giggle was always her weakness. I felt her little hands loosening the strap behind me. I didn't hesitate when I was free. I didn't know what to touch first, but I knew I needed to unwrap her. I stood, picking her up and her legs wrapped around me.

"Hang on to me, Blake," I said, walking her to a spot on the wall that I didn't think was another hidden door. I pressed her up against the mirror and felt her jump as the cool surface came in contact with her skin. "Are you okay?"

I didn't want to frighten her. She'd only had that one moment in the restaurant where things came back to haunt her from something I'd done—as far as I knew. Knowing what happened that night, I knew what might be triggers so I made sure to stay far away from them.

"I'm fine. Are you okay?"

"I'm better then fine. I just found out I'm marrying an exotic dancer." We laughed into another heated kiss. That was one of the best parts of sex with her. The talking. The playing. The teasing. It never got old.

"How do I get to you through this?" I'd been feeling for a zipper or a knot somewhere, but I was coming up short. I was practical in times like that. Sure I could fumble around like a fool, but I could ask and get inside her faster. Inside her faster was *always* the most logical route.

"Here." I pulled back a little and she pulled one end of the bow in the center. It began to unravel. I wondered if she'd mind wearing it every day. Her hands moved the silky black ribbons around her, and before I knew it,the only place it was still on was where we met in the middle. I grabbed her ass, lifting her a little, and it fell away.

She was completely bared to me. By the way her face was flushed, and her breathing labored, my girl was very turned on.

After she'd rid herself of the lingerie, she went to work on my pants. When I was free, she guided me to her entrance. It wasn't rough, but it wasn't slow either. I spun us around, taking a few steps and put her back to the pole. She stretched, grabbing ahold of it for support. She raised her arms above her head and began to lift herself onto my cock. The position allowed me to get so deep, and the weight of her body falling on me pushed me inside her in a new way. The view was amazing. Her breasts bouncing, her back arched. Legs wrapped around me moving at a pace that ensured we wouldn't be there long.

As the movements became fevered, she let go of the brass fixture and hung onto me. I wrapped my arms around her back and bent, just slightly, as I moved us both toward climax. I plunged into her, passion moving me in a rhythm more hypnotic than the music that played. She hung on for dear life and tossed her head back when she began to come.

"Don't stop," she begged. "Don't ever stop."

I never planned on it.

My favorite part of coming was the few seconds right before. The magic moment when everything got blurry and time and space stood still for us. Breaths mixed. Every fiber in my being pulled tight and then released like rain from the sky. Nothing holding it back. Nothing in its way to stop it.

I also loved when our eyes met. It was hardly every time, but when it happened it was mesmerizing. Her face filled with wonder. Passion. Awe. Love. And all for me.

When we were finally decent, or at least I was—no man needed to see Blake looking like that, all re-wrapped and well fucked—we tapped on the door she came in from. When no one came, we opened it.

"It's okay. That's my instructor," she whispered like we were sneaking out of the house in high school. The room had been abandoned and Sabrina was wiping everything down. Poles lined a long wall of mirrors.

Mirrors. Maybe Blake would consider doing some redecorating in our bedroom with mirrors. They were growing on me. First the jewelry store and now at the club. I hoped I wasn't catching a fetish. But if I was, I'd throw in a pole for good measure.

"Well, Mr. Groom-to-be, are you satisfied with our dancer's performance?"

I knew she was goading me, but what did I care? That was the best private dance of my life.

"Yes, ma'am."

"Good, I'll call you a car while your pretty bride gets dressed."

Our friends and family had left, which suited me just fine. It had been a great night. I was sure to get a lot of shit the next time I saw any of them. But the fuckers couldn't say I was a dick who blew my cash on strippers. Hell, by my estimation, if Reggie was serious about the last part of the bet, I was about two grand up for the night. I planned on collecting, even though I'd gladly pay twice for a repeat performance anytime.

I wondered how much mirror and brass I could buy with that kind of money.

Blake's parents had an early flight, and we were tired from the busy weekend. So we did what normal people do on Sunday afternoons. We ate too much food early and fell asleep watching a movie in bed. It was a really good life.

Days peeled by as the wedding crept closer and closer. I assumed shit-and-get time during wedding planning was when most men got cold feet. It was stressful, but it was nothing compared to the things we'd been through over the past few years.

We took a trip up to Seattle to see Dr. Rex, which was Blake's idea. I was happy she still felt like she could talk to someone, other than me, and I'd become really fond of her myself. She and Blake Skyped once or twice a week, and sometimes Dr. Rex would ask if I could join—particularly when the night at Grant's was discussed. But mostly it was more about Blake healing and identifying who was to blame.

Guilt was an ugly bitch and even though we slowly worked through it, there were times she struggled accepting what Grant did *wasn't* her fault. It was his. No matter what she'd done in the past, his actions were unforgivable and evil.

Dr. Rex wasn't easy on Blake either.

"What's bothering you about the wedding vows?" she asked.

"Well, it's not so much that I'm worried, it's more like I want to give him everything he wants." I was holding her hand that day as she explained how she was struggling with what to write. I knew it was because she'd already made promises to someone else and broken them. She was worried I thought she'd break ours too. Or maybe she was struggling because she didn't want them to feel repeated. It made sense to me, but honeybee was stubborn.

"Well, why don't you just find some non-traditional vows and say those? You don't have to write your own," she suggested.

"No. I want them to be personal," Blake explained.

Dr. Rex tapped her pencil against her lips.

"I've got it. Casey, you write Blake's vows, and Blake, you write his. In the past, in my opinion, that was always your biggest hurdle. You never told each other what you wanted. This is an opportunity to do that."

I liked the idea; she was a smart woman.

"I'm in," I said. "But how do we know if they're about the same, you know? Lengthwise."

Blake gave my hand a little squeeze.

"Well, I suppose I could read them for you. Or Micah and Cory, aren't they your matron of honor and best man?" Dr. Rex clapped her hands together decisively, excited by the concept.

"That's it. They can compare them for you. Oh, it's so perfect. Then you both get exactly what you want. You'll never have to second-guess that you didn't promise vows that mean something to you."

"And we don't read them beforehand?" Blake inquired.

"No. It's so romantic. The gesture of blindly promising what the other desires. It couldn't be more perfect for you two."

I was sold. Whatever she wanted, she could have. The look on my girl's face said she was on board too.

"I kind of love that idea," honeybee said. It was settled. We'd decide what promises we wanted to hear. Then we'd honor and keep them forever.

NINETEEN

Blake

Tuesday, September 14, 2010

IF CASEY THE HUSBAND was anything like Casey the fiancé, I was going to be a very happy wife. He made it easy to love and cherish him forever.

He ran errands before I got around to them. He was attentive and thoughtful. He'd made every part of planning fun, and when it was stressful, he added levity when I needed it. Truthfully, it wasn't all that bad.

The wedding was less than a week away and the dresses had been fitted and shipped to the resort. The caterers and bakers had confirmed everything was still going ahead as planned. The event hostess at the lodge called regularly and never let me worry about a package not arriving or any detail being forgotten. Everyone had their travel arrangements organized. All systems were a go for the Warren-Moore nuptials.

And sometime between then and when Casey put the ring on my finger, I quit waiting for the other shoe to drop. Somewhere over time, the fear of things going wrong faded. There wasn't anything in the world that could get in our way. I pinched myself every morning to prove it was real. I had everything I ever wanted.

I just needed to finish my vows, something Micah hounded me about nearly every day. Casey had finished his, even though Micah told me he'd changed them three times already. I think, above all else, the vows were the part I was most anxious about. It was certainly the part that meant the most.

I'd start writing, then I'd get sidetracked.

I'd think of something perfect when I was driving, but when I got home it always fell flat.

The shower. Why was it that all my good ideas happened in there and dried up faster than my hair?

It was less than a page, but if this was what writers felt when they had writer's block—I could sympathize. Fundamentally, I knew what I wanted him to vow. My requests weren't elaborate or complicated. I wanted him to love me. Always.

But hadn't he already vowed that? Proven it even? Who cared if it hadn't been said and confirmed by witnesses? How could one love a person through the hell we'd put each other through, if it wasn't an *always* kind of thing? It seemed so redundant.

I knew his vows for me were probably heartfelt and full of humor, just like him. I wanted mine to be just as meaningful. I supposed I'd know the words when they came, but they needed to hurry the hell up.

Still, the days kept peeling away.

Casey: Want to grab a drink at HLS? One last one before we're married. Seems like the thing to do.

I loved how sentimental he was.

Me: Sure. Picking me up, or am I meeting you there?

Casey: I'll pick you up. Be ready in ten minutes.

There was only one thing I needed to do before I left, but I could make it fast.

Me: Sounds good.

I waited in the drive for him to pull up, then hopped in and kissed his handsome face.

"How was work, dear?" I asked. It was his last day before we left for Oregon and then onto our honeymoon.

The past weeks had been ideal with both of us being home. I'd been enjoying working out of the local office. One of the chefs got a better job offer, so I'd been busy in the kitchen when I wasn't working on menus. I'd really missed getting my hands in there and making things for myself.

"It was good, and yours?" he answered as he backed out.

"It was great. Everything at work is taken care of. I'm pleased to inform you, you now have my undivided attention for the next three weeks." I still didn't know where we were going, but I didn't care. It was my honeymoon. With Casey. Our honeymoon. I was in good hands. Very strong, *very* capable hands.

"You gonna break down and let me get into those panties tonight?" he teased, squeezing my leg as he ran his hand into naughty territory. I didn't understand why he asked me every day. The sex-fasting was his idea. *And* it had only been two weeks. We'd gone much longer before. Plus, his rules had stipulated oral didn't count, so we were plenty satisfied. Trust me.

Leave it to him to find ways around rules he'd made himself.

"Nope. I'm off limits. You're cut off." I closed my legs to make my point.

"Wait." He slowed the car down to a crawl on our neighborhood street, looking back and forth from me to the road. "You mean to tell me I'm never going to make Blake Warren come ever again?"

"Sorry, Lou."

"God, it feels like the end of an era."

It was funny, but it was also true. Such is life. I chuckled to myself, trying to keep a straight face. "Aww. Don't think about it like that. I'm sure your wife will have sex with you."

"She better. I mean, it would be a shame to turn in a smoking hot girlfriend for a wife who doesn't wanna play with my wiener every once in a while."

"It's lucky for you that I know your soon-to-be-wife, and she's really looking forward to your … um, wiener."

"Really?" I swear he knew I was teasing, but he lit up like I'd told him something he didn't already know firsthand.

"Yep. She told me herself."

As we drove, I prayed to the marriage gods that we'd always joke like that. I prayed Casey would be telling me how different animals mate as we sipped lemonade on the back porch watching the sun go down. Laughing at our kids and how they did things so differently than us. We'd make fun of their music and clothes. Casey would probably harass any suitor to come by, regardless if it was for our sons or daughters. My silly man would probably be snapping the back of my eighteen-hour Playtex bra well into our seventies and try to race me with his walker.

This was what it was supposed to feel like. *This* was what good marriages should be. Equal parts fun and passion. Humility and love.

I stole a few glances at him as we drove the familiar streets to HLS. The windows were down, sunglasses were on, and the music was flowing.

When we arrived, it was shocking we found a parking spot right next to the door, but we didn't have to get out to see why.

"Closed? For Sale?" Casey questioned. "What the fuck?"

He dug out his phone and dialed Nate. I watched him as we waited for him to answer, listening to it together on speakerphone.

"Hey, you've reached Nate Owens. I can't come to the phone right now. So please leave a message. If this is regarding the sale of Hook, Line, and Sinker, please call our listing agent at 415-579-0811. Have a good one," Nate said in his recording.

"That's messed up. I wonder why I didn't know about this. I was just here a few weeks ago. I wonder if the office knows. " I'm sure if Aly and Nate were still dating, they did. He was genuinely disappointed and so was I.

I guess what he'd said was true. It was the end of an era.

"Well, I guess we could go home. I have packing I could do anyway."

"Yeah, me too," he replied.

Poor guy was bumming hard. It worked out for the best though, he hadn't even started packing and we were driving to Oregon the next day.

I wrote my vows the night before we left, after Casey fell asleep on the couch watching a Foo Fighters concert on television. For our last night at home as single people, it was calm and peaceful. I think he was a little solemn about the bar closing and not being in the loop, but felt like maybe the world was telling us to rest up. The next few days would go fast and we'd need the energy.

I knew I would.

The drive was quicker than expected, and when we pulled in, the staff was amazing ushering all of my wedding day things to my suite. We'd be getting ready inside, but Casey would be in a tent when everything started.

Nerves set in, but they were so welcome. It was weird how time seemed to both slow and speed up over those last few hours until I became Mrs. Casey Moore.

Everyone arrived and festivities began. We were pulled in opposite directions. The men played golf on Friday morning while the girls and I went to the spa. We opted out of a true rehearsal since the wedding was going to be pretty laid-back. There'd be no mass. No dramatic symbolic rituals. We'd planned a simple ceremony at dark where we'd say our vows and promise each other the world.

Everyone looked happy and carefree at Friday night's dinner, which was held on the lodge's property in their gigantic dining room. We didn't skimp on that. A four-course dinner. You know how I like food.

Casey was staying that night on the other end of the resort, even though he really, really, really didn't want to. Of all the traditions we'd decided to skip, that one we held onto. Mostly because we were in serious danger of breaking the pre-wedding sex-fast.

Really close.

So close he had his hand up my dress as we sat next to each other while our families toasted, or roasted us, before dessert.

"Stop," I chastised him when my mother took the microphone first. "Tomorrow." It was hard to take me seriously when I told him to quit, but made no attempt to move his wandering hand.

"I can't. I want you so bad," he murmured into my hair.

"Not long, Lou."

"We're not spending any time at that reception, just so you know."

"Whatever you say," I easily agreed. I wanted him too. "You can kiss me though."

It was chaste, but I felt the heat he was holding back behind his lips.

"How do I turn this thing on?" my mother asked like she'd never held a microphone before. Shane stepped up to help her.

"Thank you, sweetie," she bellowed as the speakers roared to life. "First I'd like to say congratulations to my lovely daughter and her handsome groom. You two make a wonderful couple. It's easy to see how much you love each other, simply by looking at you. As a mother, all you want for your children is for them to be happy, be good people, be responsible, and love with everything they have inside. My sweet Blake, not only have you become someone I'm proud of, but you've become someone I respect. You found love the hard way and never gave up. It's because of your determination we're gaining such a wonderful man into our family, and in addition, his family as well. We love you both very much." As mothers do, she got teary, dabbing the liquid emotions from her eyes with a tissue. Then she passed the mic to Cory.

"Hey everyone, if you can't tell, I'm Cory, Casey's more handsome older brother." The small crowd laughed. "I remember the first night Casey met Blake. We were meeting up for a drink the night before my beautiful wife, Micah, graduated. They say twins have some kind of connection, or something like that, but honestly I'd never felt it—until that night. I could feel how much he was into her just being in the room with them.

"It was the weirdest thing. I'd never seen Casey behave like he was. He was quiet and almost shy. If you know him like I do—well, it was obvious something was happening. The way they looked at each other that night, something sparked. Something came to life.

"If twins are born best friends, born with some unexplainable connection, then that was the night I watched how instantly theirs was going to be stronger." Cory smiled at his brother. "Whatever sibling link we have can't compete with what they have. Blake, he's a horse's ass. He's cocky. Stubborn. But he's the best friend I've ever had and it's been a pleasure watching how your love has made him a man I look up to. Congratulations."

What is it about when men get mushy that makes a heart squeeze like mine was doing in that moment?

"I'm Reggie, one of Blake's older brothers. I don't have anything prepared, but just want to say, it's a good feeling when you know your little sister is in good hands. It's a bonus when he knows how to make killer beer. I wish you a long, happy marriage."

Morgan spoke next. "Blake and Casey, thank you for letting us share this with you. I've learned a lot from my older brothers. Especially, what it looks like when a man treats a woman the way she deserves. The kind of love you two share is well worth waiting for." Morgan, more strait-laced and serious than all of the other Moore children, mouthed *I love you, guys* and blew us a kiss when she handed her dad the mic.

"Casey was a hell of a little boy. There may have been be a forest *full* of trees to climb and he'd pick the furthest, hardest one. Then he'd figure out how to climb it. He's approached life like that. Finds what he loves and goes for it. Sure, he looks like a knucklehead with all of those curls, but inside that melon of his is a brain that can find a solution to any problem. *And fast.*

He moves on instinct and passion, a lot like his mom did.

"One night when they were small, Deb and I watched the boys wear themselves out in the yard. I remember the conversation like it was yesterday. When you have twins, you can't help but compare them. Cory and Casey were always different. Anyway, we were speculating on what kinds of women they'd marry. It was easy to list things that would make Cory happy—thankfully he found all of them in Micah.

"But when we talked about Casey, we didn't know what the hell he would go for. It was hilarious. I remember their mom laughing and laughing as she told me, '*You know what? It doesn't matter what she's like as long as she lights him up. Because if she does, his world will revolve around her.*' How right she was, son. She'd be so thrilled to know you found the one who lights you up, just like you and your brother lit her up.

"Blake, we love you, sweetheart. Take care of our boy. Casey, the Moore women *always* know best. Remember that. Congratulations."

The night filled my heart so tight I thought the walls of it would collapse from its fullness.

We were so blessed. I was so thankful. So grateful. So damn lucky.

Casey walked me to my door, and we were quiet as we strolled down the hall. No rushing. I don't think we were too eager to part for the night. Just like a good book, when it's just right, you never want it to end. But I knew it wasn't a bad thing, because on the next page, the next day, I was marrying the man of my dreams. Oh, how I'd wished for him. I thought about the days when it had seemed impossible. To think I'd almost thrown it all away.

"Casey, we really made it, didn't we?" I asked when we stopped by my suite's door.

"Yeah, we did. It wasn't that bad of a trip," he said grinning. Wasn't *that* bad? It was a shame his memory was failing so early.

"Piece of cake," I humored.

"So you think you'll be able to sleep tonight?"

"It's going to be weird sleeping in separate hotel rooms again."

He moved my hair back off my shoulder and kissed my neck sweetly. I listened as he inhaled me. The print on my heart his lips made stayed even after he pulled away.

"Want me to text you to sleep, one last time, for old times' sake, honeybee?"

My lips quivered and I jumped into his arms. We held on tight. Chest to chest. Embracing everything. Our bodies. Our hearts. Our mistakes. Our pain. Our victories.

"You're my best friend, Casey Moore. I love you so much. Thank you for loving me."

Our mouths kissed, lips washing lips with affection and honesty.

"I do love you," he said as he put me down. "How about your trouble meets my trouble at the altar tomorrow?"

"Deal."

He unlocked my door for me and then puckered his lips for one more kiss before I shut it with him on the other side.

My phone buzzed in my clutch.

Casey: Don't forget to brush your teeth

tomorrow. You've had a little spinach in between your front teeth all night.

I ran to the mirror to check. Standing there, I replied.

Me: Liar. Not funny. I almost fell down getting to the mirror.

Casey: Are you still standing there?

Me: Yeah.

Casey: See how pink your nose is?

I giggled. He was such a turd.

Me: It's not pink.

Casey: Now who's a liar?

Casey: Did you know the average married couple only has sex fifty-eight times a year? That's like once a week.

Me: Or fifty-eight times in one day, depends on how you allocate your time.

Casey: I'm still afraid.

Me: We've never been average.

Casey: I hope we never are. Were you about to send me a picture of your boobs?

He never quit. I didn't send a tit pic, but I sent him one of me laying there in bed.

Casey: That'll do. You look sleepy, honeybee. Goodnight.

Me: Goodnight, Lou. See you tomorrow night. I'll be the one in the wedding dress.

Casey: God, I've waited a long time for this.

Me: Me too.

Casey: I'm so glad it's finally here.

I fell asleep smiling knowing that in good times and in bad, we'd always make it.

TWENTY

Casey

Saturday, September 18, 2010

THROUGH ALL OF OUR struggles and victories, we'd made it.

I looked at the reflection in the mirror in the small tent. Knowing she was only a few hundred feet away made me crazy. It had been the longest day of my life, but it was finally the night.

Our night.

I swallowed the lump of emotion stirring in my throat as I straightened my bow tie, took a long breath, and ran my fingers through my hair.

My hair? *Her* hair, if I were being honest.

There was no wrangling it. I thought of pulling it back into a rubber band. What if it blew in my face? What if I missed the minute she came around the corner? Because of hair? Impulsively, I considered cutting it all off. Hair be damned. I didn't want to risk not seeing her. Having a clear first view of my bride.

Not seeing her all day had sort of fucked with my head.

I hoped she wasn't too nervous. Hell, I hoped she wasn't reconsidering. There was always that chance. No. Deep down, I knew that wasn't really true. She was mine.

Officially, tonight. She'd be mine forever.

I pulled my arm out straight to expose my watch. It was seven-forty.

Showtime.

Pulling back the crisp, white flap on my tent, I was met with the men I respected the most. Men who had my back. Men who didn't mind keeping me in check. My twin, my best friend, and two men soon-to-be my brothers. Their grins created a surge of power so far inside me that I felt like I could take flight at any second.

I heard music and the low rumble of the few guests in attendance. The sound of the stream nearby trickled through my head. I blew out another breath loaded with excitement and nerves.

Shane stepped closer to me and gave my bow tie a tug on both sides.

"Are you ready for this?" he asked. His face was one-part amusement, one-part serious.

Was I ever so fucking ready for anything?

It's funny how you want one thing so bad, dream about it happening, then when something as great as this stared you in the face, you kind of wanted it all to slow down. There was nothing I wanted more, but my heart was tender knowing this was the only time I'd get to live it. Just this once. That's how you know it's important. You miss the moment before it even happens.

What if I mess up my vows? What if I miss something?

I had the promises tucked safely in my pocket, but reflexively I patted that side of my jacket—for maybe the hundredth time—to make sure all of my things were there.

Ring. Check.

Vows. Check.

I'd wondered about what she'd written for me, but I hadn't succumbed to my curiosity. I'd be making those promises blindly and wholeheartedly. Whatever she wanted of me, I'd give it to her.

Had she peeked?

"I'm ready," I answered. I was sure, but in all the excitement I'm sure I sounded anxious. And maybe I was. I wanted everything to be perfect, but that feat was almost always impossible for us. Still, there was nothing that could spoil the night and that gave me peace. We were perfectly imperfect.

Cory glanced at his watch and gave me the look that said it really was time.

Walking down the side of the chairs, which were situated at an angle. Another thing that Blake and I wanted. No sides. No mine and hers. These were our people. We shared everyone there. My stomach flipped seeing the empty seats near the front, knowing that one was for my mother.

I said a few silent words to her.

Missing out on time with you wasn't for nothing. You were right. I think she loves you, Mom. You only met a few times, but sometimes she says things or looks at things you loved and I feel you with us. I hope you're in that seat watching. It feels like you are.

When we were making plans, I couldn't envision the lights in the trees and the little lanterns that lit the aisle, but Blake had been right. The magic in the air crackled.

Like a team, with me at the lead, we took our places at the make-shift altar built of wood and covered in calla lilies. I looked down the line of my groomsmen. Cory, Troy, and Shane. When I met Reggie's eyes, he nodded and straightened his posture as the music changed.

Our wedding certainly was different. It had taken us so long to get there. We'd fought for our moment. For our life together. All painful memories of the past healed, sealed together with happiness. This was how it was meant to be. *For us.*

My father and Carmen came toward us first, walking Foster down the faintly lit lane. It was a little late for our godson, but he was hanging in there. I chanced a look at my brother. He smiled as Foster saw him and then sped up wanting to go to his daddy.

Then Mr. and Mrs. Warren walked. Blake's mom was already crying, but her smile proved they were tears of joy. He kissed the top of her head as they took their seats near us.

The gravity of everything began to swim around me. Moments and memories flooded my head.

I don't know how I'm going to do it, and it might take me the rest of my life, but I'll see to it that you and that bait of yours catch this fish.

You fill me up with so much happiness and you move me forward. NO, I go where you go. Because that's where I belong.

I likened it to the moments where right before you die, memories flash through your mind: How beautiful she looked the first time I laid eyes on her. The first time I heard her say my name. The first time I heard her say my name from pleasure.

Her tears, which I'd misinterpreted so many times, had been callouts for me when our situation had looked so bleak. How her body had wept when forced to be separated from mine.

The look of wonder on her face every time she came to climax. The flush of her pink nose.

Seeing her in a hospital bed, confessing she wanted to be my wife.

Every single fucking time she told me she loved me.

When she'd said yes.

At lightning speed, they raced through me.

Then around the corner I saw my youngest sister. Morgan was becoming such an incredible woman. Audrey who looked at the ground, smiling, followed her, but didn't look up to where we stood. I looked down at the guys and Troy's face was fixed down as well. He swayed side-to-side, then looked up at her.

She blossomed before she even saw him do it. I watched as she found his eyes and she winked. I'd never paid any attention, but things started to click in my head. Had I missed the change in their friendship? Or, had it quite possibly, already changed?

She looked at me, realizing she'd been caught. She smiled.

I'd be having a talk with her later. I didn't want her to get hurt. Not that Troy was a bad guy, but he was just so much older. He wasn't an angel and she deserved one.

But, then again, who was I to judge?

Blake only had three bridesmaids and seeing Micah turn the path that led to us, a rush of excitement hit me like a hot summer's breeze, snapping me out of my thoughts. Micah blew Cory a kiss as she walked past us and took her spot alongside my sisters.

The air smelled sweet like freshly cut grass and the lights twinkled all around. It was like a movie. Oscar-worthy, in my opinion.

The music stopped. It was so quiet I could hear the frogs bellow along the water's edge. I wasn't sure what was happening. Seconds felt like ages, but at the same time it was like my prayers had been heard and time slowed just for me.

A lone violin.

And, ironically, it was the sweetest sound I'd ever heard, the beginning bars to a song that had become more like our anthem.

The violin played. Then another. And then a third.

They walked up the aisle as their bows slid over strings and erased all the agony violins had once caused me. Then it got to the part where the lyrics started. Everyone began singing softly.

"Oh, oh, oh, oh, oh."

My heart swelled with emotion as she turned the corner and stopped. I pinched my lips together tightly, knowing if I didn't secure them they would shake right off my face.

Fireworks.

The Mona Lisa.

The Sistine Chapel.

The Grand Canyon and all of the other wonders of the world didn't hold a candle to her. She was effervescent. Breathtaking. Life changing. This was nothing new.

Our families and friends hummed all at once to our Led Zeppelin song and the sound infiltrated my skin. The trio of violins stood just to the side where there was open space.

She was the most magnificent thing I'd ever seen. She wore a long silk gown that almost looked yellow from where I stood, but it could have been the lighting. The front dipped low and was held up only by two thin strings over her shoulders. She wore her anchor next to her heart.

My honeybee. My Betty. My only.

I begged God that I could make her as happy as she made me. Hot love spread through my body and my foot bounced, instinctively wanting to run to her, but knowing I shouldn't. I needed to stay in my place and let her come to me. But somehow it just didn't feel right. Before I could stop, I was walking to my bride.

Her hair was down, but held to the side with a clip. She smiled, and her head tilted, as I worshiped her with my lucky eyes.

The heavenly violins played.

They played our song. And it was the most wonderful thing I'd ever heard.

Everyone stood and watched as I left my post. I didn't give a fuck. When it came to her, I never had. Swiftly my feet walked, but they could have been floating, I'm not really sure. I had only one focus. *Her.*

Her eyes overflowed with tears as I stopped just before her at the end of the aisle.

"I'm sorry, Blake. I know I was supposed to stay down there, but I couldn't. You're too beautiful. I had to come to you," I admitted. She didn't look upset by my unscripted move.

"It's okay, Casey." She quietly laughed. Then she moved the flowers she was holding to her side and offered me her free hand. I moved to her side and took her small hand in mine; then lifted it to my heart.

It was weird and strange and everyone looked at us as we stood together at the bride's entrance, but it was also exactly perfect.

We were going together. *We've got this.*

She wasn't a possession to be given to me. There was no exchange needed. But something wasn't right about her walking alone either. She'd decided she didn't want her father walking her down the aisle a while back. After I spoke to him, he understood. But there, in the moment, every instinct I had said *don't make her walk alone*. It was completely the opposite gesture to commemorate what we had. What we'd been through.

What *she'd* been through. And I was about to promise to be by her side forever. Starting out, by her side, felt like the only thing that was right.

"I'm glad you came over," she whispered. "I'd gladly walk to you alone, but walking together is better." So in sync. She understood my intention so well. Loved that woman.

The violins played.

This time my heart listened.

Four feet, sure and steady, walked our souls to the Promised Land. That may seem dramatic, but I can assure you it was not. In front of us was everything, the vows were our beginning. They were the starting line, and it was finally our race to be had.

Then we were there, watched by the supporting eyes of our loved ones.

At the head of the altar, we stopped and faced each other, but we didn't part. We stood face to face, fingers locked and pressed to my chest. There was no reason to feel territorial about this woman, as no one was competing with me. It was a weird feeling. I was possessive, only because I wanted her to feel it. She loved my claiming and I'd show her every day that I wanted her for my very own.

"Hello, everyone," said Dr. Rex. "I'm so honored to share with Blake and Casey in this special ceremony." As she began talking, we pulled—only slightly—away from each other to let everyone watch the doctor as she spoke. "When they asked me to officiate, I had my reservations. I'm not holy. I'm not a very religious woman. What could I offer?"

Blake watched Dr. Rex with a lovely expression of pride on her face. Yet another decision that made this wedding feel like *ours*. Not like the repeat of someone else's. It was stamped with Betty and Lou like our mugs from so long ago. Just like us.

"For those of you who don't know me, I'm a doctor. A scientist of sorts. I review information. I study. I question. It's in my nature to dissect issues people have and formulate a plan. A goal. A way.

"As you all know, the scientific and faith-based communities hinge on what they perceive as fact. But Casey and Blake fall into both in that respect. So if some consider this union religious, I'd have to agree. But I also see it as a beautiful example of science and one of the Universe's most wondrous gifts. Observing their love is marvelous in person."

My bride's thumb rubbed back and forth over my hand and my breath hitched, as the moment caught up with me again. Her eyes said, *"Look at us. We're here. We really do have this."* She beamed.

I hope the photographer listened to my instructions. Catch *all* of her smiles.

"There are many theories on amour, on human chemistry, on marriage and husbandry throughout all species. There are animals who, without faith of a higher power, find their biological mates. The reciprocal to themselves. And they monogamously mate for life. That is fact," she stated.

We'd shared many conversations with her about how we wanted the ceremony to happen. What we were comfortable with—what was important to us. It was probably just as unorthodox as the rest of our relationship had been.

Neither Blake nor I felt like religion was the center of our vows or our commitment, but we both felt like it was certainly a higher power that had brought us first together, and then gave us strength to fight. Unquestionably, however, there was something so basic—so chemically fundamental—to our attraction.

"When I first met Blake, and she told me her story, I was so curious. Skeptical, too, in fact. Surely, she was in love. It was obvious. The way she spoke of the man in her heart. The way her love made her glow, even when she felt less than a prize to be had.

“I had to see for myself.” Dr. Rex chuckled. “This love-sick woman. I hoped—for her sake—he felt the same way. Then I saw him with her, unfortunately, in a hospital, she didn’t even know he was there. He was tender and attentive. He was just as tangled up with her as she was him.”

I winked at Blake when she stole a sideways look at me.

“So, call it what you will. Divine intervention. Chemistry. God’s will. Casey Moore loves Blake Warren. And she loves him. Undisputedly. Unapologetically. Unconditionally. Untamed and completely.”

At that point, I was watching Blake as she listened. She’d sucked in her bottom lip and I would have given anything to hear her thoughts. Hear what she was thinking.

“Blake and Casey have written vows for each other. Perfect for them. Giving blindly and wholeheartedly they are making promises to one another. They consent to each other’s needs. They yield to the other’s will. And after all, isn’t that what we want from love?”

Dr. Rex opened her arms and then kindly asked, “Blake, would you go first?”

Her brown eyes shimmered. Gone was worry. Gone was guilt. Only hope and trust and love were reflected. I knew what she was about to say, as I’d written them myself. But I never expected how overwhelming it would be hearing my wildest fantasies spill from her wedding lips.

She giggled when her trembling hands unfolded the paper I’d handwritten her vows on.

“I, Blake Gretchen Warren, take you, Casey Frances Moore, to be my equal partner in love, ally through conflict, accomplice in mischief, and lover for the rest of my days on this Earth." She read slowly, it was clear she hadn't broken her word to wait until now. "I promise to always include you in my joys and my trials, my happiness and my sorrows. I promise to always let you share my burdens and ask for help when I need it. I promise to never serve you steak on a paper plate." She laughed through the most beautiful tears I'd ever had the pleasure of seeing. "I promise to never willingly share my cheesecake, but make you work for it. I promise to always be *your* Valentine, *your* Betty, and *your* honeybee. I promise to always be careful when you're not around because I carry your heart in mine." She stopped when the words choked her. Finally she continued, voice wobbling, chin quivering. "I promise to always let you catch me, always follow the wind back home to you at night, and trust that you'll always chase me and welcome me home. I've been yours from the first night we met, and you've been mine that long too. I promise that even though love is hard work, it's worth it. I love you and I promise to never stop."

I've never in my whole life wanted to kiss two lips more than I did in that moment. She was mine.

When she finished, she put the words to her heart and said only to me, "I took the bait." My knees almost failed.

Dr. Rex said, "Casey, now you, please."

I pulled the paper from my pocket and took a deep breath.

TWENTY-ONE

Blake

Saturday, September 18, 2010

I WANTED HIM TO kiss me so badly. It felt like his lips were pulling mine toward him, but I had to wait. He stood, trembling like I was. He was vulnerable and sexy and more than I'd ever expected to get out of this life. He was mine.

He winked at me again and I almost fainted, then he began.

"I, Casey Frances Moore, take you, Blake Gretchen Warren, to be my lover, my best friend, and my wife. I vow to always kiss you good morning and good night. I promise to always make you laugh and never filter what I'm thinking from you. I will always tell you what I want, even if I'm not sure you want to hear it. I promise I'll always keep our home happy and safe. I promise to never hurt you, never lie, and never throw away my red pants." His smile was so bright and it took top seat above all the millions of Casey smiles fluttering through my mind. "I promise that I'll always challenge you, always trust we can do anything together. I vow to never cut my hair shorter than the approved length and to make sure my phone is always charged. I promise when times are rough, we'll get through them. I promise when times are perfect, I won't take them for granted. I promise I'll love you forever and make that as long as possible. I promise to always be your Lou and that you'll always be my honeybee. I promise I'm yours as much as you are mine, today and for the rest of our lives."

It was quiet when he finished. It was peaceful in that space and time where we were the only ones who existed. I couldn't take my eyes off him.

"You, their people, are witnesses to this union and their pledges to each other. I challenge you to help them remember these promises, if they should ever forget. It is my pleasure, by the power vested in me by the beautiful state of Oregon, to announce this love permanent and these two people wed, bound and tethered together by the law and by their free will.

"Everyone, Mr. And Mrs. Casey Moore," she proclaimed. "Let the groom kiss his bride."

There are many fairy tales that speak to the potency of that very moment. Two lives joined in matrimony. I can assure you there was never a bride in history more in love than I was with my groom.

I'm sure our family cheered. I'm sure they clapped and some probably cried.

But when his two warm hands cupped my damp cheeks and claimed me in front of God and everyone, it felt like the most sacred kiss of my life. It was better than our first kiss. Better than the second. It was the sum of all our kisses multiplied by every ounce of passion and affection I'd ever felt. I embraced him, my husband, and didn't hesitate to kiss him back.

Our mouths moved as one, as brief as it seemed looking back, but the taste of that kiss will live somewhere inside me for the rest of my life. It was sweet and salty from our tears. It was his gentle tongue insisting on sampling me, so swiftly it came and went. Knowing we were being watched, but having no desire or willpower to stop it. The moment took over and we both surrendered.

He held tightly like he was trying to push me through his skin. If it were possible, I would have gone.

Then it turned into pure bliss and we laughed together as the sounds and smells of the night drifted back into our reality.

We were married.

"Thank you," he said into my hair as we walked, hand in hand, past our loved ones. "I've never been this happy."

"I hope I hear you say that again and again."

We took pictures and cut the cake. I threw the bouquet; he tossed the garter. We ate. All the while, through hugs and handshakes, I watched as a passion grew in Casey's eyes. Our physical relationship had always been strong. Our bodies always knew they were mates. Our souls were linked stronger than blood. Stronger than our wills. Stronger than the trials we'd overcome.

I danced with my father and he danced with his sisters.

We had *our* first dance and claimed a hundred different new songs to call our own.

Everything was exponentially better being his wife. Food tasted richer. The air was lighter and swirled around us like the fizzy bubbles in a toasting flute. There were so many stars, and they were brighter than they'd ever been.

My skin felt new to his touch. Everything had changed, when I thought it would all be the same. That we'd already achieved the goal. I was wrong. There *was* more. He never left my side for more than a minute, and when he did, he always had one eye on me.

Shoes came off. Bow ties, too. Formal wear made casual as the night grew to an end.

"Have you had your fun, Mrs. Moore?" he asked as we swayed to a song I'll never remember, but will nonetheless never forget how it felt.

"I think I have. Do you mind taking your wife to bed? She needs you."

His eyes closed and he bit his lip smiling. "That's the sexiest thing you've ever said to me." And before I knew it, I was swept off my bare feet and in his arms. He gave me a light toss to situate his arms and announced, "Good night, everyone. It's been fun."

They laughed and kept doing what they were doing, as if the party wasn't in danger of spoiling without us.

He walked with purpose. A man on a mission. My cheeks hurt from smiling.

"Can you reach in my pocket, Betty? Our room key is in there." I reached in and pulled it out as he slowed at our door. "Go ahead, I'm not letting go." I slid it through the reader and opened the door to our room. Only one light on the far side lit the space. I didn't mind though. We had no need for modesty. We loved each other's bodies.

He walked us to the bed and then sat down, still cradling me in his arms.

"This is the best night of my life," I admitted, knowing the *true* best part was yet to come, and my fingers roamed his face needing to touch him. He didn't say anything back, but his response felt like he was agreeing. His hand moved up my leg, my dress falling open at the slit that went clear up to my hip. He kissed my neck and I laid my head on his shoulder allowing me to savor his gentle touch.

"You smell so new to me. You taste different, too," he said as his lips found my jaw. "Why does this feel so different?"

He was right, and I couldn't explain it either.

His fingers touched my lips. "Were you always this intoxicating?" His voice was hushed and low. My husband's eyes studied my mouth like he'd never seen me before.

He moved, setting me on the bed and stood in front of me. "Sit up for me, honeybee."

I got to my knees before him.

"Lift your arms, please."

He took his time finding the zipper on the side and pulling it down. He gathered the fabric of my wedding dress and slowly pulled it over my head. I hadn't worn a bra. It wasn't a dress that called for one. I only had a tiny, satin thong, but I was unashamed. The more he studied me, the more beautiful I felt. He ran one finger up my thigh and over my stomach. It traced my collarbone, over the ridge of my shoulder and down my arm. Every hair on my body shot out to greet him.

He hypnotized me. My breaths were coming in uneven waves.

He took two steps back and began unbuttoning his shirt, discarding it when his fingers ran out of loops to empty. His hair looked just like the night we'd met. Perfectly chaotic. Totally him. I watched as he licked his lips and the action sent a pool of arousal to my core. My body screamed. *Taste me, too.*

He pulled his undershirt out of his flawlessly tailored dress pants exposing his lean chest and stomach to me. The muscles below his ribs flexing as the cotton passed his head.

He unzipped his pants. My chest caved under the sensual pressure in the room.

"There's no past anymore, honeybee. Only our future. Only firsts," he said, allowing his pants to fall to the floor before stepping out of them. "What are you thinking about?"

"How this is the first time I've had sex on my wedding night. Like I'd saved it for you all along."

He smiled so proudly like I'd handed him the world.

"It's the first time I'm going to make love to my wife," he boasted.

I knew I had an even bigger gift and prepared to watch him receive it.

"It's the first time I've ever had sex with my husband …" I said, and committed that very second to memory, then finished, "… pregnant."

It was the most spectacular rainbow of emotion. The small gasp. His mouth fell open. The shock matured into pure joy, spreading from the corners of his eyes down his face like a waterfall. My Casey. My love. My words had hit him like a bolt of lightning. I watched him hear them.

It was so fun that I did it twice. Because sometimes things happen that are so far past fantastic you have to do them again simply to see if they're as spectacular the second time. Those precious moments are almost as good as the next, when you learn sometimes second-time moments are *more*.

"We're having a baby, Casey," I said. Was it hormones fueling my emotions, or my emotions amplifying my hormones? Regardless, it was splendid. It took him down on his knees. The poor things gave right out. I giggled as he braced himself on the mattress in front of me, grinning like a mad man. Then almost as if a switch flipped, it rocked him and he started to tear up.

There were a few moments during the ceremony earlier when I thought he was about to lose it, but he never quite did. It was a moment shared between just us, in a hotel room, on our wedding night, in our underwear that stole the show.

"You're having my baby?" he said in disbelief.

"I am."

"You're giving me a baby," he stated and it sounded like he was testing it out.

"Yes."

"Like right now? Not *let's make a baby*?" He sniffed. "Like we already made one and it's in here?" He tapped a soft finger at my belly.

"Uh-huh," I answered.

"We're having a baby? You're giving me a baby." He crawled up the bed and I inched back to give him room.

"You gave *me* a baby."

"You surprised me," he admitted, out of breath. The shock made his body tremble and I felt it as he laid us back on the mattress.

"You surprised me too. I didn't know you were doing that."

"I wasn't kidding. I was *really* putting babies in you."

"Uh, yeah you were," I agreed.

He kissed me and it only intensified when I turned my head to deepen it.

"Thank you," he said around our lips. "Thank you so much. You married me. You're giving me a baby. You've given me everything."

I hoped for all women's sake that his reaction was typical, because it didn't get any better than that. Everyone should get to experience that kind of happy.

The fever in his kisses increased and I felt his excitement change to arousal. My hand found him, hard. I gripped his length and he moaned into my mouth.

He bewitched me.

His arms surrounded me as we lay side-by-side, touching and exploring as if we couldn't already write the manual to each other's bodies.

His hand cupped my tender breast. Squeezing like they were brand new to him.

I slipped my hand under the waistband of his silk boxers and teased as he moved in and out of my grip. His fingers traveled south and my whole body sunk into the plush pillow-top mattress when he put his hand on me. My bones turned into liquid and I felt like I could slip through the bed to the floor. As much as I wanted to please him, when he took control of me, my focus faded like fog as the sunshine melted it away.

"I really get to keep you. All of you. These are mine," he said before he sucked a fortunate nipple into his mouth.

"And this is mine." His long finger parted me. I swear I felt every ridge and line in his fingerprint as one by one they pressed. He put pressure where I craved it, working my body like a marionette doll. A touch here and I arched. A feather-light graze there and my fingers dug into the sheets above my head. A flick and my toes curled.

What little control I had was blown away like delicate seeds off a dandelion in the wind.

I was somewhere else, and when I came back to us, he'd taken off my panties, and his boxers were kicked off as well. I held onto his face, and he hitched my leg up his side; his erection needed no guidance, and our hips moved together in one motion into one another.

"Oh, you feel so good, Casey," I whimpered on an exhale when he was completely inside me. I pushed against him more to see how close we could fit. "I want you. Only you. Forever. I'm yours forever."

Our wedding night was something indescribable. We'd already said all of the words. Thought the thoughts. That night we just felt each other, communicating with each other by touch. He gave me what I needed, no holding back. All speech reduced to murmurs and moans, our names the only words that made any sense.

We didn't even get up when we were finished to straighten up the bed, get water, or brush our teeth. We were sated just as we were.

I fell asleep listening to his heart beating slowly and his shallow breathing, tucked into his arms where I belonged.

TWENTY-TWO

Casey

Sunday, September 19, 2010

THERE WAS NO PLACE else in the world I'd rather be. My wife was in my arms.

Our wedding had been flawless. Best day of my life.

But our wedding night was something completely different. I'd expected ravenous sex and arms and legs everywhere. After the reception, I wanted to consume her. There was a feeling inside me to claim her like I never had before.

Then everything changed.

She was having our baby.

I'm not saying my passion went away, or I didn't want to fuck the hell out of my brand new bride—I did. I probably always will. But it was different. I was different.

It wasn't about getting to a climax because I already felt like I was there. Her telling me I was going to be a father was the single biggest rush of my life. It was the best gift. The biggest present. The most valuable thing anyone had ever given me. I was blown away.

"When did you find out?" I asked her the next morning. The sun was just coming up and she was looking through the room service menu.

"Only earlier this week. It was killing me not to tell you. I had to drink shitty sparkling cider all weekend. I wanted it to be special." Mission accomplished.

"It was. I almost passed out." She tossed the binder aside, rolled over and perched her head on my chest. I'd been laying there staring at the ceiling for a while. I remembered when Cory told me about them being pregnant and how freaked out he'd been at first. I didn't feel anything like that. Of course, we were a few years older than they were then and we were married—just barely. Kind of.

"Are you still happy about it? It's not too soon?"

"Yes, I'm happy. I was shocked, but honeybee, this is the best thing ever. We're having a baby. Our very own little person to play with and teach and dote on. I couldn't be happier. Seriously." It was the truth.

There wasn't one negative thing I could think of. Sure, some couples like to wait awhile and get a house or spend more time together first, but all of that was bullshit.

We had a house and having a kid would only make it worth more to me. In one night my attention had shifted. My priorities had changed. Somewhat.

I still loved what I did, but I didn't want to be away from her—especially now. It would make me a lunatic thinking I was missing something or not there when she needed me. I had a lot of thinking to do.

"Good, because I'm really excited. It didn't even freak me out, Casey." Her eyes got glassy as she stared out the window. "All I could think was, everything just keeps getting better. You know? Like maybe everything we went through, all of that crap from before, was a price we paid for all of this. Like we'd done our time or something."

I understood what she was saying. Sometimes I felt like that too.

I said, "Yeah, like the past two weeks when I couldn't have sex with you made last night so fucking good." My analogy was weak, but it was the same thing when you boiled it all down. Bad times helped you realize how good the best times are. They give you perspective. Teach you how to appreciate what you have.

"Yeah, something like that." She snapped out of whatever daydream was floating around in her pre-coffee daze. "I'm hungry." She hadn't had her post-coital snack last night. I bet she could eat one of everything on the menu. I was starving too.

We ordered omelets, fruit and coffee and when that wasn't enough, she ordered some oatmeal and orange juice to top it off. She said that she'd have to start cutting back on coffee, but not today.

There wasn't much we had to do before we left on our honeymoon, and I'd intentionally not booked our flights until Monday, hoping we'd stay all day in bed.

I'm a smart man because we did just that.

We didn't watch T.V. We didn't leave the room. The only time we left the bed was to answer the door for food and once to take a shower. I rediscovered all of my favorite places on her body and let her explore mine.

If that first day as man and wife was an example of how our life would be, I'd never have to worry about some dumb married couple sex fifty-eight time average I read.

We were only on day one and had five tick marks on the calendar. I wasn't keeping count, per se, but it was hard to miss a tally like that.

Sex or no sex, though, the next year would be pretty damn exciting.

TWENTY-THREE

Blake

Monday, September 20, 2010

WHAT A WAY TO start off our first year married. Pregnant and going to the last American frontier. I was on to him; he wasn't fooling anybody.

"Alaska, Casey?" I asked for the ninety-fifth time as we boarded our flight.

"What?" he asked innocently. "You make it seem like a bad idea. Neither of us has ever been."

I knew better. We weren't just checking a destination off some arbitrary bucket list. He wanted to ensure we were having sex more than the typical fifty-eight time average that year. Taking me to some cottage in the wilderness would be a sure-fire way to do it. There was no way I was going to outrun a bear. Or a wolf. Or any other wild animal that was frolicking around. He had me right where he wanted me. He was a genius, but I'd never let him know that.

"Fairbanks isn't like the middle of nowhere," he reminded me. "They have indoor plumbing and everything."

Turns out that indoor plumbing came in handy. Where the first night and day was spent eating and exploring the cool city, then driving to our cottage, day two found me in the bathroom of said cottage until around noon.

"Are you all right?" Casey brought me a 7-Up as I sat on the floor in front of the toilet.

"Yeah, I think so."

"That shit is serious. How do you feel?"

Who knew morning sickness started so soon? I thought I'd have a few weeks to get used to the idea. I'd only known for less than a week.

"I feel fine right now; it just happens all of a sudden."

He set the drink down on the counter and offered me a hand up.

"Do you think we should call a doctor or go home early?" Casey had been on his phone all morning googling how to combat my symptoms. I was going to learn a lot that day if I didn't start feeling better and occupy his time. The more he read, the more anxious he got.

"No. We're on our honeymoon."

"Yeah, but you're barfing every thirty minutes. One website

said that as long as you're not feeling crampy, morning sickness is actually a sign of a healthy first trimester."

He was speaking in trimesters and he'd only known for three days. All in Casey's world was alive and well. Full-steam ahead.

"I'm pretty sure I'll be barfing no matter where we are. We might as well be shacked up in a real shack," I teased. Our cabin was nothing remotely close to shack-like, but it was fun giving him shit.

"Blake, this place has a movie theater. It's far from primitive."

Carrying the soda with me, I walked back into the master bedroom and climbed back into bed. "I'm sorry I don't feel good this morning." Even though he'd brought up babies on more than one occasion, and I'd only thought about them in theory, finding out I was pregnant made me unconditionally happy.

"Shut up. You still look hot. And if you're hunched over the toilet, you're an easy target if I want a little doggy action."

"Ew, you wouldn't."

"No. I wouldn't," he confessed. "Some people are into that though. I bet I could find us a movie to watch later on that big screen, if you're curious."

He plopped down next to me and perched his head on his hand. Casey looked fine in anything, but the way his pajama bottoms hung low on his hips and his T-shirt fit just so, well let's just say he had casual down to a science. His presence made the yuckiness bearable. I wasn't alone and he was my favorite thing to look at.

And so began our honeymoon routine.

Mornings were rough, but by the time lunch would roll around, I'd feel right as rain. If you have to be sick with someone, I'd suggest finding someone who could make you laugh. He was a master at distraction.

"Is it too early to pick out names, honeybee?" he asked from his spot on the bathroom floor. After you do the same thing five mornings in a row, you find your places. I leaned against the tub and he against the wall facing me. Mostly we just looked at our phones and talked about the wedding, or how it had been a dumb idea to come all the way to Fairbanks.

I laughed at his question. Was it too early? I didn't think so. I'd already been racking my brain too.

"I don't think so. What do you have in mind?"

"I think we should name him Ringo." I waited for the telltale Casey smirk that usually followed when he was kidding. And I waited. Then I threw up and waited some more. I'd like to hope my non-answer was answer enough.

The names he thought up were preposterous at best. It was easy to tell he found inspiration quickly, and impulsively he'd throw them at me. "Janet? Ms. Nasty? No, never mind that one. I hope it's a boy. Those names are easier."

Our honeymoon wasn't even close to ruined by the shitty mornings. Looking back, the pukey-bathroom-floor mornings were some of my favorite memories of the trip. I got pretty good at toilet paper basketball. One morning he brought up an instructional video of how to fold washcloths and towels into origami. We played Name That Song or rather I lost at Name That Song. Who in the hell would guess "The Fabulous Thunderbirds"?

We didn't tell people about the baby for a while and it was our fun little secret. Casey bottled a couple cases of root beer in Bay Bottles for me at work and when we'd go to visit his dad and Carmen or Cory and Micah came over, I'd drink those as to not raise any suspicion. It felt like we were Russian spies hiding a secret love child in plain sight. Those were his words, not mine.

"We could call her Nakita," he'd suggested. Then he bared his teeth to look fierce.

"Veto."

"For a boy? Like Danny DeVito?"

He was such a smartass, but I loved it.

The morning sickness hung around a lot longer than I'd like to admit, but we got through it.

As the months got cooler, I got fatter but I didn't care. Casey worshiped my body, always curious about how I was feeling or how I was changing as our little one grew.

"Maximus. That's a good name." He looked hopeful that time. I didn't mind Max, but you shouldn't name your child based on what you watched on Netflix. We could do better.

"Veto." I denied him, like always, as we cooked together the night before Thanksgiving. It was the first holiday we were hosting in our home. We planned to tell everyone the news then and calling whoever couldn't make it. We weren't finding out the gender until it came out. Casey said it was too much fun guessing and he didn't care either way as long as he or she had my smile. I hoped whoever had his.

I chopped vegetables for stuffing and baked piecrusts, and he cleaned up as I went.

"So do you think they'll accept our offer?" I asked him.

He finished chewing the celery he'd stolen and nodded. "Yeah, I think so. I think they like knowing it's going to still be a bar, you know? It's not like we're tearing it down and putting up a parking garage." He had a point. We'd never tear down Hook, Line, and Sinker.

What had been a pipe dream on the bathroom floor in Fairbanks turned out to be attainable. He was going to keep his portion of Bay Brewing, but he wanted to build something that was ours. I wanted to be in our restaurant, not just make plans for other people's. I was a chef; he was a brewer.

My whole world began in that bar. The first time I made him smile. The first place he called me honeybee. Our first kiss was on those bar stools. Our first dance on the old wooden floor. There was no conceivable way we could let something unfortunate happen to it. That place held a special spot in our hearts.

So, we were buying it. As long as everything went through.

"I have a name for that too," he informed me as he circled my waist and placed his hands on my little belly bump.

"Hit me."

"The Two Ships."

Now that was perfect. "I love it, Casey. That's it."

It was moments like that when it was hard to believe we were ever not on the same course. When things clicked into place. When everything worked out as if it had been in the plan all along.

"It's going to be a lot of hard work, honeybee. Are you sure you want to do this?" I think we were both a little apprehensive. We had a baby on the way. The next few months would be full of meetings with contractors and doctor's appointments, but it felt right.

"I'm sure. I really want it."

"Then that's what we'll do. The Two Ships it is."

I turned around in his arms and kissed my husband. I think every business deal should be made like that. I hugged him and did my best to show him how much I loved him.

Around the dining table with his dad and Carmen, Troy, Micah, Cory and Foster, Audrey and Morgan, Casey announced, "Happy Thanksgiving. Honeybee is having my baby."

"Oh shit," I sat up in bed and held my stomach.

"What?"

"I just felt it." It was the weirdest sensation. A quick rolling flip of a movement. I'd been waiting patiently. We'd heard the heartbeat and we'd had the sonogram, but it didn't feel real until that second. "Casey, I felt the baby move."

There was no way he could feel it, but he put his hand beside mine anyway. Then it did it again. A dull tickle on the inside. It was magnificent.

"Did it hurt?" Always worried, always concerned. He'd taken the vow to protect me seriously. A little too seriously at times, but I let it slide because he was him.

"No. It felt cool," I explained as I lay back into the bedding. It was our first Christmas morning together. After all the absent years, it was the first one we were going to share. "What time is it?"

He rolled to his side and lit up his phone. "It's about five thirty. Merry Christmas."

"Merry Christmas," I repeated and snuggled close to him. Our tree was overflowing with presents. We had a lot of time to make up for and a new little someone to buy for, which made it fun. We'd wrapped the many things we'd bought for the baby's room. I wasn't due until June, but it was hard not to.

"Do you want to get up and open stuff?" he said with one hand cupping my ass. "Or do you want to stay in bed for a little while?"

One thing about being pregnant, I was horny all the time. He never complained, telling me it was his job to make sure I had everything I needed. That included him. I fought my Christmas curiosity and chose to stay in bed with the sexiest present I'd ever received. I answered with my mouth kissing his chest.

"I love Christmas," he said.

I love Christmas, too.

Days passed, months passed, and we found a rhythm.

I remember him telling me once he wouldn't be satisfied until we were sleeping on the same pillow and fighting over stupid things. All of those things that seemed like shots in the dark were our dreams come true.

"Can you take this trash out?" I asked as I waddled around the kitchen. I could take it out, but my feet were so swollen from the night before. Our soft opening at The Two Ships. It had taken us about five months to get it open and I'd really wanted it up and going before the baby came. The night went off without a hitch. We didn't have the brewery part quite up to speed yet, but the restaurant side was going to have a strong start.

"Yeah, why don't you go sit down, Momma?"

He doted on me. Hand and foot. It was hilarious how *he'd* had cravings, but I hadn't. The only thing that really grabbed my attention was something I couldn't have.

"Yeah, and could you get a beer?" He'd stocked our house with ice cream and pickles and every kind of cheese you could imagine, but it was beer I craved.

He laughed, knowing the drill.

After walking to the curb and washing his hands, he found me on the couch and brought my favorite Porter with him in an ice-cold pilsner glass. I watched as he took a long drink and placed it on the end table. Then he kissed me.

Just the taste of it on his tongue was enough to pacify my craving. I looked at it like a win-win. Beer and Lou. It was a delicious combination.

"My genes are strong, honeybee. That baby likes beer." I giggled because it was true and my big fat belly bounced.

"Don't you? You know the good stuff." He slid his hand in my shirt, like he did every night, and talked to the baby as it did flips on my bladder. His voice always caused movement, so it seemed they were already a pair I didn't stand a chance against.

TWENTY-FOUR

Casey

Tuesday, May 17, 2010

I DIDN'T STAND A chance against Blake and that baby. They had me right where they wanted me. Around their tiny pinky fingers. Becoming a husband and then finding out I was going to be a father, was like someone saying you won a brand new car, and free gas for life, and an island in the south of France, and a mansion, and all the beer you can drink, and blow jobs on the hour.

Okay, it wasn't quite that obnoxious, but it was good.

Blake was incredible and every day I found new reasons to

love her. When I watched her try three times to get her shoe on because she couldn't bend around her big belly. When I made her laugh and she held her crotch to keep from peeing. When it took her two tries to roll over so she could wrap an arm around me in the middle of the night. My heart wasn't just full, it was growing.

The house was alive with projects to get done before the baby came. A crib to put together. A room to paint. Shelves to hang. But I was too busy watching her. We'd bought Hook, Line, and Sinker and turned it into our dream jobs. I'd be making beer, hands on, and I could change it up whenever I felt the whim. The best part was we could work together.

No more solo road trips.

No more good-night texts.

No more missing her. Ever again.

It was perfect, too. I had my space in the building, which we'd expanded to accommodate the kitchen and microbrewery. She had her zone and I had mine. But we could ride to work together and at night when one of us was buried under, the other was there to help.

I'd watched my girl transform as the pregnancy progressed. After we made it through morning sickness, her belly seemed to pop out overnight. Thin shiny lines striped her skin where she stretched to hold our baby. At first I think she was a little embarrassed of them, but I thought they were bad-ass. They were like self-creating tattoos.

Her boobs got huge and a little aggressive, I might add, but I knew how to stay out of their way. Her rosy nipples had darkened, bringing a new reason for me to study them.

As time passed and the baby's due date came closer and closer, it got more uncomfortable for her to sleep, and when she wasn't working, eating or sleeping, she wanted to be fucking. I didn't know pregnant women were so insatiable and unapologetic. I'd never heard, "Fuck me, Casey," so many times in my life as I did in that nine months. She blew the fifty-eight times average right out of the fucking water in the first trimester. I was sort of proud.

It had only been that week when she'd lost some interest. She was napping more and cleaning non-stop. Micah said she was making a bird's nest or some shit, but her restlessness was freaking me out.

We'd just fallen asleep when I felt her jerk and hitch her legs up to her stomach.

"Ow. Ow. Ow," she panted.

I knew that sound. I was there when Foster was born, but we were still about three weeks until D-day. I flipped the light on and she was sweating. Just like I'd seen Micah do. Teeth bared and that crazy look in her eye.

"Blake, are you all right?" I'd been gently scolded yesterday. All I did was worry about her. About the baby. I was kind of losing my mind. Thing is, being overprotective isn't a choice. I was innocent, but I was getting on my own nerves at that point.

Still, she'd never made that sound before. She'd never looked like that.

"No. Ow. No. Ow."

We didn't even have the bag packed. The fucking bag wasn't ready. I wasn't ready. She was in labor and I was already fucking up.

"What can I do?"

"I don't know. Ow."

Casey, get your shit together. This is not a drill.

I sprang from bed and started throwing things in a duffel bag. Clothes. Her iPod. Shower stuff. I grabbed some clothes for myself. I made sure I had cash in my wallet. I found shorts, and slipped on my tennis shoes.

"Blake, what do you need, baby?"

"Don't call me baby. Oh my God, my water just broke."

Everything was going too fast. *Water was breaking.* I knew we were forgetting everything we'd read we should expect.

"I don't know what to do," I said as I started pacing.

"Ow. Come here," she told me. I sat down next to her and she grabbed my hand. I thought it was sweet until she damn near broke it. "Casey, listen to me. We can get stuff later. Ow. We need to go now."

Stuff later. Go now. That made sense.

I helped her stand up and she found her legs, although they didn't seem so sturdy.

"Can you grab me some new pants and a bra?"

I went to the closet and found what she needed. I helped her dress and I tossed the wet clothes in the bathroom on our way out.

She took a few steps, then she'd stop. I rubbed her back. I felt so damn helpless.

When we were in the car, I felt better. I felt like I could do something. Driving her to the hospital was my purpose. The dashboard said 1:50, so I guess we actually had fallen asleep, it just didn't feel like it.

Did I tell you how fast everything was going?

I dialed the number I had programmed in my phone under *Go Time*.

"Hello, labor and delivery," a female voice answered. "This is Janel."

"Janel, my wife is in labor. We're coming in." I said quickly. I didn't want to be on the phone long. There wasn't a lot of traffic, but I needed to drive. I had more than my boner and cheesecake to protect.

"Okay, what's her name and who's her doctor?"

"Blake Moore and Dr. Garcia."

"All right, how far away are you?" she asked calmly.

Didn't she understand we were having a baby? Then again, she did this every day.

"I'll be there in five minutes." I wished it were faster though. At that point, Blake was breathing and hanging in there, but I could tell she was in a lot of pain.

Janel chuckled. "Okay, Mr. Moore. Drive safely. We'll be down there waiting for you."

She wasn't joking. When we pulled into the lane, a nurse was waiting for us. I slammed the car in park and ran around to help Blake out as the nurse came to us with the chair.

"Mr. Moore, you can park your car around the side of the building. Have the desk let you up to the third floor. Someone will tell you where we are when you get up there," she instructed.

"No. I'm not leaving her. Fuck that car. They can tow it," I stated. No fucking way was I leaving her.

"How will you bring baby home without a car? It'll only

take you a minute."

Blake winced as another set of contractions hit. I saw her zone out and focus. She was a lot different than Micah in labor. Blake was a quiet fighter, where Micah almost murdered me. I was kind of expecting it to be more like that.

"Casey, please go park. It will only take a minute. Please." She drew a long breath in through her teeth. Pulling the car around didn't sound so bad when *she* asked me.

"Okay," I said and kissed her. "I'm right behind you."

I whipped that motherfucker into the first spot I came to that wasn't designated for every other person on the damn planet. Doctors. Emergency patients. Inpatient. Outpatient. I just needed a spot.

Then I sprinted back to through the doors.

"Three, please," I said to the person working the desk. She buzzed the doors open for me to pass on my way to the elevators and I rode up. The damn thing was slow. I'm pretty sure I heard the whole Michael Bublé Greatest Hits album in my ride. It took that damn long.

I walked off and found another nurse sitting at a desk.

"I'm Casey Moore. They just brought my wife up. She's having my baby." The last part was redundant, but it just came out.

"She's right down this hall in room 315."

My mind flashed back to the night we met.

Honeybee: Room 315.

But I didn't stop to write it in my journal or anything. I had shit to do. She was having my baby.

The room was already busy. There were two nurses getting

her hooked up to stuff and starting an IV.

"So your water already broke then, Mrs. Moore?"

"Yes, just before we left. It happened suddenly," Blake said as she inhaled through her nose and out her mouth.

"Okay, I'm going to check to see how far we are along."

I found a spot and stood next to Blake as the nurse examined her. It had taken about nine months for me to get used to that. It was awkward having someone else touch your wife.

In that moment, I just wanted them to say everything was fine and then they'd make her feel better. We'd decided drugs were the way we were going. Blake didn't want to be really out of it, and she'd said if she could handle it she'd do it that way, but there was no question she was in a lot of pain and about to take what they gave her.

She reached for my hand and I bent down to her ear.

"You're doing really good, honeybee. I'm right here."

"Well, you're dilated to four centimeters, but it seems like baby has moved around. Did they notice baby was turned around at your last appointment?"

"No. Dr. Garcia said everything seemed fine last week."

"Oh, everything will be just fine." We both listened, hanging on every word the nurse said. "I'm going to call the doctor and let him know how you are. I'm sure he'll be here very soon." She moved the gown Blake had been changed into down, and pulled the sheet up over her legs.

"What does that mean?" I asked nobody in particular.

"I think the baby is breech, Casey. I thought I felt something weird the other day, but I just thought it was a big kick or a flip. This kid is always moving." She didn't sound worried as she said it. It was a good thing one of us was trying to stay calm. Her eyes said otherwise, though. "It'll be okay. Let's just wait for the doctor. Talk to me."

Talk to me.

"Did you know this is room 315?" I asked her.

She shook her head no.

"That was your hotel room number the night we met."

"It was?" She smiled.

The poor woman was in labor and I made her smile. My life had just been made.

"Yep, I remember thinking how pretty you were. How out of my fucking league you were, but I wanted you so bad."

She tensed and pushed a hand into her stomach like I'd been seeing her do the past few days and she rolled on her side toward me. I pulled up the chair and let down the rail so that we were face to face.

"You were so hot, pretending to want to talk about beer, all the while *drinking* my beer."

"It's good beer."

"It *is* good beer. I really was going to break up with Aly in person that night, but I didn't want to leave after we met. After I met you."

"You were being a jerk," she said. "You didn't want to talk to me."

"Yes, I did. I just couldn't figure out what to say, and I hoped you'd come back over to talk to me."

"I did," she said on an exhale. "I think we have a good story, Casey."

I leaned in and kissed her lips. "I think so, too."

"Would you do it all again?" she asked.

I thought back on the pain, the laughs, the hurt and the anger. I contemplated it. Weighed it all up, pros against cons. There was only one answer.

"In a fucking heartbeat."

Blake was right. Our little one was breech and raring to come out. We sat on one side of a blue curtain while they pulled our baby from her. We couldn't see anything, and I wasn't about to look, so we stared at each other waiting. My honeybee, wearing a hair net and a pink hospital gown, was radiant. I loved her even more.

"It's a girl!" We heard one of the nurses say.

Those elongated minutes, while the doctor and nurses worked, were like standing on the edge of a cliff. Then hearing her wail, as she took her first breath, was the jump.

She screamed bloody murder.

It was the most exhilarating moment of my life. I cried like a girl, but that wasn't so bad. My wife was a girl and, man, was she bad-ass and our daughter would be too.

My heart grew new chambers and filled with fresh blood and purpose.

Then our little girl screamed some more.

They held her up so we could see her. She was pink and

white and her mouth was huge. And open. And loud. Her little chin quivered and the nurse pulled her away to do whatever they do to babies right after they're born.

I kissed my wife over and over again. How was I ever going to repay her for giving me such an incredible life?

The doctor stitched her up and moved us into a different room while they waited for Blake to recover a little more. It was sort of nice. The hustle and bustle was dying down and it was only us for the first time.

"What should we call her?" Blake asked, in a new voice I'd never heard from her. It was her mommy-voice and I liked it. It was low and sweet and soft. It came naturally like most things do for her. I'd been suggesting names for months. None of them were ever any good, but nevertheless I was throwing something she could swing at.

There was one name I'd been thinking about that I hadn't mentioned. It was more of just a word that made me think of her, even before she was born.

"Wake," I said. "Wake Elizabeth Moore." It was a long shot. I'd suggested far more normal names, which had all been respectfully shot down.

"Wake," she rolled it around on her tongue, testing it out. "Why Wake?"

"Because that's what she is. After everything. After all this time. She's what we made. She's the result. Through rough storms and calm waters we kept moving. Our love kept us going forward and it made the perfect wake."

EPILOGUE

Casey

Present Day

"DADDY, TELL ME THE one about Lou and the honeybee again," Wake requests as we are getting her all snuggled down for the night. She loves when we read to her at bedtime. But most of all, she loves when we make up our own stories. Little does she know her favorite one is true. Well, kind of.

We skim over a few parts.

"You like that one the most, don't you?" I pulled her covers tight around her.

She's tenacious. Wild and curious. Wake has my hair and Blake's big brown eyes. She has all of my favorite parts of her mom really. She's gentle and has a big heart. She forgives easily and always wants to do the right thing.

"Yes, I like when Lou gives the honeybee the angel's ring. When he sur-poses to her. It's so sweet, Daddy."

"*Pro*-poses. And I like that part, too." I clicked off the overhead light and turned on her lamp, then took my seat on the bed next to where she lay.

"Okay, once upon a time, a long, long time ago. Lou fell in love with a honeybee, but the world wasn't ready for their love just yet ..."

As I told the embellished, kid friendly version—including the big, bad robot and the phone stealing witch—she begins to drift off. She bats her heavy eyelids, just as they draw closed for the night, fighting to hear her favorite parts.

Blake waddles in and crawls into the bed beside our little girl. Her big belly hanging out from under her tank-top.

We're having a boy this time. My wife gives me everything. I'm *such* a lucky man.

Our baby girl falls asleep, but I finish the story.

"... and then they lived happily ever after." Only, that part isn't true. It's just what little girls want to hear. It's a PG-rated fantasy and I think it's dumb.

Happily?

How generic. How underwhelming. The truth is much more ... powerful. Life with her makes the blood pound harder in my chest. Makes every minute worth remembering. Makes working hard and building a life for my family a privilege. Certainly all that is better than *happily*.

My honeybee gives me the most beautifully content smile.

"I love you, Casey," she whispers so Wake doesn't hear.

"I love you more, honeybee."

You see, we live arguing and annoyed. We live passionate and insatiable. We live with love that grows and multiplies. It's taking out the trash and it's compromising. It's fucking on Saturday night and making love on Sunday morning. Pushing buttons. Learning different ways to make her smile. It's never the same. Our love startles us and keeps us on our toes. Our love is easy, but we have to work at it. Because it's worth it.

Never perfect. Never expected. Never finished.

And it was never handed to us.

Because once upon a time a curly headed boy named Casey walked into a bar and found his whole world sitting on a stool and he didn't quite know how to handle it. And once upon a time a smoking-hot young lady named Blake offered him some trouble, not knowing what she was getting into.

So, fine, if the story of *Lou* and his *honeybee* has to end with happily ever after, whatever. But the story of Casey and Blake doesn't.

That's not quite good enough for us, it sure-as-hell doesn't do our love justice.

I'd like to suggest they fucked each other's brains out enthusiastically forever. Or they loved the shit out of each other so much until the end of time.

Or, maybe, they just … *loved on*.

ACKNOWLEDGMENTS

For this book, I'd like to acknowledge the readers who've loved these two characters even when they shouldn't have. You're a tough bunch. You never give up on love and, for that, I respect you. All of the ladies in the Mo Stash and Take the Bait have a piece of my heart.

I have to thank my beta readers, Megan and Bianca. Your feedback and thoughtful encouragement through all stages of this book have been paramount. Blake and Casey are the couple they are because you've challenged me to give them my best.

Also, a heartfelt thank you to Jessica, Natasha, Fiona and Candy.

A sincere thank you to my cover designer, Hang Le at By Hang Le; my editor, Marion Archer at Marion Making Manuscripts; my proofreaders, Erin Noelle and Lori Sabin; and my formatter, Stacey Blake at Champagne Formats. You are a good team.

I'd also like to show my gratitude to reviewers and bloggers who read, generously share and promote my work. It humbles me. Thank you.

To my author friends who let me bounce crazy ideas off of them, who keep me focused and motivated, who never let me have a day where I feel alone in this. Thank you for your support, your knowledge, and your friendship. Aly, Erin, Meghan, Laurel, Nat, Tara, Chelle and so many others in the amazing groups I snuck into. It's awesome knowing and experiencing this with you.

To my friends, family and neighbors for understanding why I'm not around as much while I chase this dream.

To my husband, Danny for being the best assistant and partner around.

To Casey and Blake, who can't read because they don't exist, but I need somewhere to put this … you've taught me a lot about myself. You've made me tougher. Smarter. More resilient. And I'll fucking miss you so much.

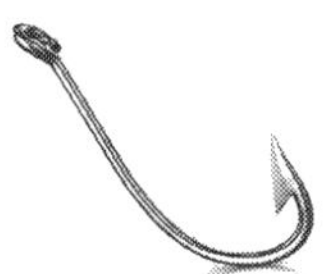

Made in the USA
Lexington, KY
11 November 2015